# BLACK AND WHITE

ERIC WALTERS is the highly acclaimed and best-selling author of over sixty novels for children and young adults. His novels have won the Silver Birch Award and the Red Maple Award, as well as numerous other prizes, including the White Pine, Snow Willow, Tiny Torgi, Ruth Schwartz, and IODE Violet Downey Book Awards, and have received honours from the Canadian Library Association Book Awards, The Children's Book Centre, and UNESCO's international award for Literature in Service of Tolerance.

To find out more about Eric and his novels, or to arrange for him to speak at your school, visit his website at www.ericwalters.net.

# Black and White

# White

## ERIC WALTERS

PUFFIN
CANADA

PUFFIN CANADA

Published by the Penguin Group

Penguin Group (Canada), 90 Eglinton Avenue East, Suite 700, Toronto, Ontario, Canada
M4P 2Y3 (a division of Pearson Canada Inc.)

Penguin Group (USA) Inc., 375 Hudson Street, New York, New York 10014, U.S.A.
Penguin Books Ltd, 80 Strand, London WC2R 0RL, England
Penguin Ireland, 25 St Stephen's Green, Dublin 2, Ireland (a division of Penguin Books Ltd)
Penguin Group (Australia), 250 Camberwell Road, Camberwell, Victoria 3124, Australia
(a division of Pearson Australia Group Pty Ltd)
Penguin Books India Pvt Ltd, 11 Community Centre, Panchsheel Park,
New Delhi – 110 017, India
Penguin Group (NZ), 67 Apollo Drive, Rosedale, North Shore 0745, Auckland, New Zealand
(a division of Pearson New Zealand Ltd)
Penguin Books (South Africa) (Pty) Ltd, 24 Sturdee Avenue, Rosebank,
Johannesburg 2196, South Africa

Penguin Books Ltd, Registered Offices: 80 Strand, London WC2R 0RL, England

First published in a Puffin Canada paperback by Penguin Group (Canada),
a division of Pearson Canada Inc., 2009
Published in this edition, 2010

1 2 3 4 5 6 7 8 9 10 (OPM)

Copyright © Eric Walters, 2009

LIBRARY AND ARCHIVES CANADA CATALOGUING IN PUBLICATION

Walters, Eric, 1957–
Black and white / Eric Walters.

ISBN 978-0-14-331250-5

I. Title.

PS8595.A598B53 2010     jC813'.54     C2009-905247-4

Visit the Penguin Group (Canada) website at **www.penguin.ca**

Special and corporate bulk purchase rates available; please see
**www.penguin.ca/corporatesales** or call 1-800-810-3104, ext. 477 or 474

*I look to a day when people will not be judged by the colour of their skin, but by the content of their character.*
——Dr. Martin Luther King, Jr.

# Black and White

# *CHAPTER ONE*

"SO, ARE YOU GOING to stay or what?" Steve asked.

"I really don't want to," I answered.

"Come on, Tom, school's over and you've got nowhere you have to be. So you can stick around and watch a little basketball, right?"

"I don't want to watch basketball."

"That makes no sense. You *always* want to watch basketball," he said.

Steve and I were best friends, and teammates—not just on the school team, but on the rep team as well—and we did spend a lot of time together around basketball.

"But the *girls'* team?" I questioned. "Do I really want to watch our girls' basketball team play?"

"Hey, basketball is basketball, and I never thought you'd get tired of it. Are you feeling all right? Should we take your temperature?"

Steve made a big show of reaching up to check my forehead, but I blocked his arm.

"Besides, they're pretty good," he argued.

"The Homelands Middle School girls' basketball team?" I asked. "You really think they're good?"

"Well … maybe not. But what I *do* know is that some of those girls stayed after school last week to watch us play against Hillside."

"That's different. Our team really *is* pretty good. Besides, if you're talking about Kim, she didn't stay to watch our *team* play, she stayed to watch *you* play."

"Well … if you think about it, I practically *am* the team," Steve replied.

"Yeah, *right*," I said, sarcastically.

"Okay … but you have to admit that, except for you, I am definitely the best player on the team."

"Not to mention the most modest, the most humble …"

"Fine. So why don't you stay anyway? Watch the girls play and keep me company."

"And then what?" I asked. "Is your mom coming to drive us home?"

"Well … I was hoping that maybe your mother could drive us."

Suddenly a light went on in my head. "So *that's* why you've been bugging me all day to stay and watch. You don't want my company, you just want a ride home."

"I'm insulted!" Steve said. "You're my best friend. Of *course* I want your company." He paused, and a big smile crossed his face. "And if I get a ride home as well, that's just a bonus!"

"Aha! And what if my mother can't give us a drive home … would you still want me to hang around?"

"Of course. It's a long walk home and I'd enjoy your company. Come on, Tommy, stay … be a pal, and I'll owe you big time."

I didn't answer right away. I wanted him to squirm a little bit more.

"Well …?"

"I'll call my mother. If she can come pick us up, then I'll stay and watch the girls play."

Steve slapped me on the back. "Thanks, I really appreciate it."

"But if she can't, then I'm going right home. Right? No way I'm walking all that way."

Steve looked at his watch. "You'd better hurry then, 'cause the bus leaves in less than five minutes."

When I got to the office I walked in and stood in front of the big counter, trying to catch the secretary's eye. She was sitting at her desk, talking on the phone, like I wasn't there. I always got the impression that she didn't really like kids, as though we were some sort of inconvenience that got in the way of her real job——running the school. I was pretty sure that was her job, because it didn't seem like either the principal or the vice-principal was in charge. However, it was obvious from her end of the conversation that this wasn't any sort of official school business she was discussing. She was talking about a movie she'd seen.

I looked at the clock over her head. The bus was going to leave any minute. I didn't have time for this conversation.

"Excuse me," I said.

She turned so her back was to me.

"Excuse me!" I said even louder.

She turned back around and scowled at me.

"I need to use the phone," I explained. "I have to call home."

Her scowl grew even darker, but then she nodded her head and turned back around. I pushed open the little swinging gate and circled around behind the counter. I picked up the phone, pushed the button on the only open line, and quickly dialled out. The phone started to ring. It rang again … and again. *Come on, Mom, be home …*

My mother picked up the phone at last. "Hello?"

"Hi, do you think you could come and pick me up from school in about an hour?" I blurted out.

"Why are you staying?"

"There's a basketball game that—"

"You forgot you had a basketball game?" she asked, sounding shocked.

"I don't have a basketball game. I'm watching a game … the girls' team is playing."

"I didn't know you had an interest in girls' basketball," she said. She sounded amused.

"I'm interested in *all* basketball," I protested. "So, can you come and get me or what?"

"I guess so. You'd better get going now or you might miss the faceoff."

"Faceoff? Mom it's a——" I stopped myself mid-sentence as she started to laugh.

"I know, I know, it's a tipoff. I'll see you in an hour or so."

"Thanks, Mom ... see you then."

I replaced the phone in the cradle and looked up at the secretary. I was going to thank her, but she had her back to me, the phone still glued to her ear.

I circled back around the counter, left the office, rushed down the hall and into the gym. I got there just as the clock was ticking down the last two minutes before the start of the game.

Our girls were at one end of the gym, in two rows. One row was taking layups while the second row was grabbing the rebounds. It was a pretty standard drill. Of course, it would have looked a bit more familiar if they'd made more than an occasional basket. They really weren't doing very well. Some of them were downright brutal. They were going to get killed today.

Steve stood up in the bleachers and waved for me to come over. It wasn't like I was going to have any trouble finding him because the stands were practically empty. There were maybe fifteen students, a couple of teachers, and a handful of parents there to watch.

As I walked across the gym floor I saw the other team warming up. They were doing a shooting drill. They put up a few shots—wide, short, long, but nothing that dropped. They didn't appear to be any better than our girls. Maybe this wasn't going to be such a blowout after all.

I settled in beside Steve as the buzzer sounded. Most of the players hurried to their respective benches while a girl from each team, the captains, huddled with the ref at centre court.

"Your mother okay to drive us home?" Steve asked, a bit anxiously.

"Would I be here if she wasn't?"

"I guess you're right. So, what do you think about the team?"

"From the little I've seen there really isn't much to say."

"Go easy on them, Tom. It's school basketball. Think about the guys on the boys' team. There really aren't more than five or six guys who can really play ball."

"Maybe not, but at least there are five or six," I said. "That's not happening here."

"Some of these girls can play," Steve replied.

"Like who?"

"Just watch and you'll see for yourself."

The ref blew his whistle and the starting five from both teams came out. They lined up and decided who was covering each man—or player, I guess—and then got ready for the tip. One of the girls from our team went into the circle. She wasn't even close to being the tallest on the team, so why was she taking the tip? The other team's centre had to be half a head taller. The ref tossed the ball up and our centre leaped up into the air, sailing well above the outstretched hand of the other player. She tapped the ball forward to one of her teammates, who tried to grab the ball, but it slipped through her fingers and then bounced off the legs of another player and right back into the hands of our centre! She put the ball on the ground, dribbled upcourt, and laid it in for a basket! The bench and the few spectators in the stands cheered.

"So," Steve said, "do you see anybody who can play some ball?"

"Who is she?" I asked.

"Her name is Denyse."

"How come I don't know her?"

"She's in grade seven."

That explained it. I knew everybody in grade eight in the whole school, but only some of the sevens. Steve, however, knew everybody. His mother always said she wished he'd spend half as much time on his homework as he did on the phone and on Facebook.

"I didn't think they let grade sevens on the senior team," I said. "They wouldn't let *us* try out for the grade eight team last year."

"They don't usually, but she's so good they had to."

The play went back up the court to our end and the Hillside guard put up a hurried shot. It bounced off the side of the rim, through a couple of hands, and then right into Denyse's grasp. She grabbed the ball with both hands, stuck out her elbows, and swung her arms around to protect the ball. As everybody cleared away and started back up to the other end she put the ball down and began dribbling.

"Is she the centre or the point guard?" I asked.

"She's whatever she wants to be," Steve said. "She can play every position."

Denyse brought the ball upcourt, and three members of the other team came toward her. She feathered a pass through them to an open teammate right under the basket, who fumbled it, regained it, and then wildly tossed up a shot that clanked off the backboard and into the hands of the other team.

I watched in fascination as the play went back and forth up and down the court. It was obvious that there was nobody out there who was even in the same league as Denyse. She could stop anybody one on one, while there weren't even two members of the other team who could work together to contain her. The only reason the score stayed close was that she spread the ball around, setting up teammates, even though they failed to convert her set-ups and sometimes couldn't even catch the ball. Just as impressive as her play was the fact that when somebody did blow a play she didn't yell or make a face or give them a dirty look. That was something I'd been working on with our team. So far, I'd had only mixed results. I hated when people did stupid things on the court and sometimes I had trouble not letting them know, right there, right then.

"You know who she reminds me of out there?" Steve asked.

"Who?"

"You."

I smiled. "She does play pretty well," I said, trying to not sound too smug.

"I don't mean the way she plays—although I suppose there is a resemblance there. I mean the way she looks."

"You think she looks like me?" I asked, a bit shocked.

Steve nodded his head.

"Well, Steve, if you haven't noticed, I'm white and she's black. I'm male and she's female. I'm about five ten and she's about five inches shorter. Just how do you think we look alike?"

"The face."

"I don't look *anything* like her."

"Yes you do," Steve argued. "You both have that same expression on your face when you play."

I looked at Denyse as she came back down the floor. I didn't see any particular expression ... she just looked ... looked ... determined ... no, more than that, she looked angry.

"That's how you look," Steve said.

"I do not," I protested.

"Yes you do, and believe me, I know that a lot better than you do. You're on the inside of that expression, but I'm the guy who spends most of the game staring at it from the outside. That's *exactly* what you look like."

I wasn't really sure I agreed with what he was saying, but there wasn't much point in arguing. So what if I looked angry, or determined? That wasn't bad, was it?

"So, do you think you could take her, one on one?" Steve asked.

"Don't be stupid," I snapped. "Of course I could take her."

"How about her brother?" he asked.

"Of course I could take her ... who's her brother?"

Steve laughed. "You don't know anything, do you?"

"I know that you're starting to sound a lot like a gossipy girl."

"So, I guess you don't want to know ... ?"

I didn't answer.

"It might help if you knew her last name. It's Smith."

"That really helps. There must be more people called Smith than any other name in the whole world, and ... wait, you don't mean Jamar Smith, do you?"

Jamar was two years older than us. He'd been in grade eight when we'd come to the school in grade six. He was on the basketball team back then. Heck, he *was* the basketball team.

Steve laughed again. "Can't you see a little bit of his game in her?"

"Not really. They don't play the same. Heck, they don't even *look* the same."

"What did you expect?" Steve asked. "A grade seven girl who's six foot five?"

"I don't know. I just didn't know he had any sisters."

"One sister, two older brothers."

"And how do you know all that?" I asked.

"Me?" Steve said, pointing a finger at himself. "I'm just a gossipy girl, remember? Besides, who doesn't know about the Smith brothers?"

I guess in some ways he was right. Practically everybody in our part of town who knew anything about basketball knew about the Smiths. The two older brothers were at university on basketball scholarships, and Jamar was supposed to be better than either of them were at his age. He was already on the senior team at Erindale High School, even though he was only in grade ten. Not that he *looked* like he was in grade ten. He was already one of the tallest guys, and he had to weigh at least two hundred pounds.

The Smiths lived a few blocks over from me. Sometimes I'd walk by their house, and there was always a basketball game going on in their driveway. I really would have liked to join in, but I didn't know those guys, and they were all at least a couple of years older than me. And way bigger. And a lot better, too.

The buzzer sounded to start the fourth quarter. Our team was now up by twelve points—or, to be more accurate, Denyse was up by twelve points. She was the entire team. I'd watched her the whole game, and not just because the ball was always either in her hands or about to come back to her. I couldn't take my eyes off her. She was so skilled ... so fluid ... so cat-like ... so ... *pretty*. Despite the scowl on her face—apparently the scowl I shared with her—she was really, really good-looking. And a couple of times when the play stopped, when she smiled, her whole face lit up. One of those times she'd looked up at the stands, like she was looking right at me while I was looking at her. We'd both quickly looked away.

"Kim looks pretty good out there, don't you think?" Steve asked.

I looked over at him. "Steve, she's on the bench."

"I know that."

"She's been on the bench almost the whole game."

"I know that, too."

"And when she was on the court I don't think she touched the ball even once," I added.

"Not once," Steve agreed.

"She actually kind of looked afraid of it, and ..." I paused. "You weren't thinking about her basketball skills, were you."

There wasn't much doubt what Steve was thinking about.

"She looks so *fine* in that Homelands uniform. It just makes me proud to be a student here."

I couldn't argue with that—Kim really was good-looking—but the last thing Steve needed was any encouragement to talk about girls. We'd been friends since grade four, and he'd always been a little bit girl-crazy, but over the past year he'd stopped thinking with his head completely and let his hormones take over.

"Hey, there's your mom."

She'd come in through the double doors at the far side of the court. She smiled and gave me a big wave. I slumped down in my seat.

"At least she didn't blow you a kiss," Steve said.

That was only a little bit funny. I could see her actually doing something like that.

The year before, my mother had stopped working. She'd said she wanted to get off "the treadmill" and spend more "quality time" with us ... which was kind of a scary idea. There were benefits, for sure, though. I liked her being more relaxed. I also liked her being able to pick me up from school or drive us places. And my lunches were certainly a lot better. What I didn't like about her being around more, though, was that she was around a *lot* more. She did volunteer work at the school, and she was one of the handful of parents who sat in the stands every time our team played. I guess I should have been happy—and I'd never let my mom know

I wasn't—but what thirteen-year-old guy wants his mother hanging around all the time?

"Hello, boys," my mother said as she settled into the spot right beside me. She leaned over and gave my arm a little squeeze. "I didn't know you two were so interested in girls' basketball ... or is the interest more in the *girls* than the basketball?"

Steve chuckled, my mother smiled, and I did neither. I just stared at the game in progress in front of us.

"So, Steven, is there one particular young lady on this team you're most impressed with?" my mother asked.

"Well ..."

"Wait, let me guess," she said. My mother looked very intently at the players, first those on the floor and then those sitting on the bench.

"I can't make out her number, but I think it might be the one sitting on the bench, third from the left."

"That's amazing!" Steve said, nodding his head. "You're wasting your time stuck at home—you should be working for the psychic hotline!"

"She's not psychic," I said. "She's just using her head."

"What does that mean?"

"Try using *your* head for a second."

"No way," Steve said. "It's painful enough having to think all day at school."

"Do you want to explain it to him, or should I?" I asked my mother.

"Be my guest."

"Fine. Kim has long blond hair, blue eyes, and she's tall and thin."

"Believe me, I've noticed," Steve said.

"That's what you always notice," I said.

"What does that mean?"

"It means she looks like the last girl you liked, and the one before that, and the one before that, all the way back to the first girl you kissed in grade five."

Steve shrugged. "I guess I am sort of predictable."

"And which girl do you like, Thomas?" my mother asked.

I shot her a dirty look.

"He's had his eye on Denyse," Steve said.

"Shut up, Steve."

"Which one is she?" my mother questioned gleefully.

"Number four, on the floor," he said. "She has the ball."

"Oh! I can see why you'd like her, she's very pretty and——"

"I *don't* like her!" I snapped, cutting her off. "I don't even know her! The only reason I've been watching her is because she's the only person on the whole court who knows anything about——"

The buzzer sounded, cutting me off and ending the game.

"Okay, let's go," I said, getting to my feet.

"Do you have all your homework?" my mother asked.

"Of course I do," I said, holding up my backpack.

"How about your gym clothes?"

"They're in my locker, where they always are."

"Where they've been for weeks. It's time to wash them," she said.

"More like time to *burn* them," Steve said.

"They're gym clothes. This isn't a fashion show," I protested. "Some of us should be a little less concerned about how we look."

"And some of us should be a little *more* concerned about how we *smell*," Steve replied.

"And all of us should be concerned about heading home and having supper. Let's get going," my mother said.

# *CHAPTER TWO*

I OPENED MY LOCKER and grabbed my gym clothes from the bottom. As I untwisted the ball of clothes to put them in my backpack I caught a strong, nasty whiff. Okay, maybe Steve was right. I stuffed them in the pack and did up the zipper to seal the smell in. And then I remembered that I had left part of my lunch in there, hoping to nibble on it on the drive home. Suddenly I didn't feel so hungry.

I slammed the locker door closed, clicked the lock in place, and then hurried down the hall. I exited out of the doors leading to the parking lot and—darn—Steve was already at the car, sitting in the front passenger seat. I hated being in the back seat. So did Steve. We always fought about who'd get the front. I'd hoped he'd still be saying goodbye to Kim so I could get there first.

As I approached the car, Steve gave me a little wave, accompanied by a smirk. I knew what the smirk meant. For a best friend he really could be a jerk sometimes.

I tried to open the back door. It was locked. The front driver's-side window glided down and my mother poked her head out the window.

"Judging from what Steve said, I think it might be better if you put that pack in the trunk," she suggested. She flipped a little switch and it opened. There was no point in arguing. I tossed the bag in, slammed it closed—hard— and circled back around, climbing into the back seat.

"Okay, let's go," I said.

Mom put the car into gear and we slowly circled around the parking lot, went up the drive-way, and came to a stop at the busy street, waiting for a break in the traffic.

"They really should put in a traffic light," she said.

"My mother won't even try to hang a left here," Steve said. "She just turns right and then circles back around the block."

"That might be smart, but I think I'll wait it out and take my chances ... say, isn't that that girl Denyse across the street?"

I bent forward slightly so I could see out through the windshield. It was her, standing at the bus shelter.

"Looks like she's waiting for the bus," my mother said.

"Probably the eighty-one," Steve said. "That'll take her up to South Common, and then she'll catch the bus that goes along Folkway."

"Folkway?" my mother questioned. "Does she live in our neighbourhood?"

"Two streets over from you, on Plowshare," Steve said.

"On Plowshare ... does she live at the house where they're always playing basketball in the driveway?"

"Yeah, that's the one," Steve said. "Is this more evidence of your spooky psychic abilities?"

"No, it's just that she obviously plays basketball, and there really aren't too many black families on Plowshare."

"I don't think there are *any* other black families on that street, are there?" Steve asked.

"Maybe not. Her family certainly keeps that property in nice shape. They have a beautiful garden that I've admired for a long time."

"Personally, I admire the basketball court," I said. "Must be nice to have a big, flat driveway like that. And they have a great hoop and backboard. They've even painted on the lines. It's amazing!"

"Have either of you ever played on that court?" my mother asked.

"Not me."

"Me neither," Steve added.

"Well, why don't you two just go over and ask if you can join in?" my mother said.

I had to roll my eyes—it was such a mom kind of thing to say, like we were still kids sharing toys in preschool.

"They would never let us play," Steve explained.

"Why not?"

"They're older than us, and bigger, and better … a lot better."

"But isn't that how you get good, by playing better players?" my mother asked.

"If they *let* you play," I said.

"The only way to find out is by going and asking. What have you got to lose?"

*Oh, I don't know*, I thought. *Our pride? Our dignity? Our teeth, if they thought we were being rude?* I was about to answer when the car zoomed forward into a break in the traffic. We rocketed across the lanes and then, just as suddenly, came to a stop right in front of the bus shelter! What was she doing? My mother hit the power window button on the passenger side and the window slid down.

"Hello!" she called out to Denyse, who was standing right there beside us. "I'm Mrs. Martin, and I guess you know my son, Thomas, and his friend Steven." Steve waved. "We're driving right by your house and I was wondering if you wanted a ride?"

I glanced up at Denyse. She looked embarrassed and confused. I felt embarrassed myself.

"I know you shouldn't accept rides from strangers, but we're hardly strangers," my mother continued. She flashed a big, friendly smile.

Denyse didn't move.

"You'll get home in fifteen minutes instead of fifty ... that bus can't be a very fast way to get around."

Denyse stepped forward, opened the door, and hopped in. I jumped across the seat and out of her way.

"Thanks," she said. "I appreciate it."

"Put on your seatbelt and let's get going," my mother said.

I heard the belt snap shut and my mother put the car into motion. We drove along in silence for a while. I felt really awkward ... what was I supposed to say?

"That was quite a game you played today," my mother said, breaking the silence.

"Thanks ... did you see the whole game?" she asked.

"Just the last quarter," my mother admitted, "but Thomas told me you were easily the best player on the court."

I felt myself suddenly start to blush.

"Yeah," Steve added, "he told *me* that you *really* impressed him."

She turned to me. "Thanks, I appreciate that."

"That's okay," I mumbled.

"Do you spend a lot of time playing with your brothers?" my mother asked.

"Hardly ever," she said. "They don't want to play with me because they're older and they think I'm not good enough for them."

"You certainly looked good enough to me," my mother said.

"Her brothers are really good," Steve said.

"Better than you and Thomas?" my mother asked.

Both Steve and I broke into laughter. Denyse didn't say a word; she was being polite.

"You don't understand, Mrs. M. Denyse's brothers—they're pretty much basketball stars!" Steven exclaimed.

"Yeah, they can play some ball," Denyse said. "They're almost as good as they *think* they are. But you two could keep up."

"You've seen us play?" Steve asked.

"Sure. A couple of games for the school team, and once at a rep game," she said.

"You've seen our rep team play?" I asked in surprise.

"I caught part of one of your games," she said. "I got there early to see one of my brother's games during the tournament a couple of weeks ago."

"Did we win?" Steve asked.

She shook her head. "But I did see enough to know you both had a good game."

"That was so nice of you boys to stay and watch the girls' game today," my mother said. "I don't suppose they get the support that the boys' team gets."

"And that's exactly why we came," Steve said, "to support their fine players."

"I'm sure the girls really appreciated it," my mother continued. "Right, Denyse?"

Denyse shrugged. "Sure ... I guess."

We drove along in silence for a while. That wasn't exactly the answer my mother had expected.

"So what are you boys up to tonight?" my mother asked.

"We were planning to go to the movies," I said. "To Silver City ... to see *The Long Way Home*."

"Is that movie *appropriate*?" my mother asked.

"It's not restricted or anything, if that's what you mean," I said. "I think it's 'adult accompaniment.'"

"And just what adult is going to accompany you?"

"That's where I come in," Steve quipped. "I'm nearly an adult."

My mother laughed. "And how are you *nearly* adults going to get to and from the movies?

I think you'll at least need an adult to accompany you in the car."

"Well ... we were sort of hoping that a very kind and wonderful adult might drive us there," I said.

"Did you have any particular kind and wonderful adult in mind?" she asked.

"Mom?" I asked. "Could you please drive us to the movies?"

"What time would we have to leave?"

"We were thinking about going to the late show," Steve said. "I'm not really sure when it starts."

"Nine-fifteen," Denyse said.

I looked over at her.

"And it ends at ten-fifty-six."

"How do you know that?" Steve asked.

"I looked it up. I'm going to see the same movie tonight ... that is, if I can get a drive from my parents."

"Looks like I'm going to be driving there anyway, so I could drive you as well, if you want," my mother offered.

"I wouldn't want to put you out," Denyse said.

"You're only a couple of streets over, so it's not really out of my way."

"But I'm going with a friend."

"Does your friend live far away?" my mother asked.

"Not far ... actually, she's coming over to my house for dinner," Denyse said. "But I really think I can get a ride from my parents, so thanks for the offer, but it's okay."

"Well, if you can't, just give me a call and I'll pick you and your friend up."

"Thanks, that's very nice of you," Denyse said.

"Write down our number for her, Thomas," my mother said.

"My pack is in the trunk, remember?"

"You can just tell it to me," Denyse said, "and I'll remember it."

I said the number. I was awful at remembering numbers but it was obvious that Denyse wasn't, because she repeated it back to me perfectly without a mistake.

We turned onto Denyse's street. I could see her house, and on the driveway—as usual—there was a basketball game in progress. There were six guys playing a game of three on three. They were all big guys ... high school players.

"Just pull up in front," I said. "Don't go into the driveway."

"I wasn't planning on knocking anybody down," my mother said.

"I just don't want you to disturb the game, that's all."

"Thanks for the ride," Denyse said as she climbed out of the car.

"Call if you need a lift tonight," my mother reminded her just before Denyse closed the door.

Denyse walked right up the middle of the driveway and the game stopped. One of the players started to talk with her. My mother put the car into motion and gave the horn a little honk and waved. Denyse turned around—actually, all the guys on the driveway turned around—and she gave us a smile and a little wave. I slouched down slightly in my seat.

"She seems like a very nice girl," my mom said.

"Quiet, though. She's as quiet as you are," Steve said, turning around in his seat.

"I'm not quiet," I said.

"Yes you are," he argued.

"Nope. I'm just waiting for you to stop talking so I have a chance. Besides, there's nothing wrong with quiet. You might want to try it sometime."

We turned off the street, made a fast left, and were on Steve's street.

"You don't have to stop," Steve said. "Just slow down and I'll—"

"Tuck and roll," I said, cutting Steve off. It was a running joke between us because our parents were always complaining about having to drive us from place to place. We pulled into Steve's driveway.

"Thanks for the ride, Mrs. M.," Steve said.

I climbed out of the back seat as Steve climbed out of the front so I could take his place.

"We'll pick you up around eight," I said. "I want to make sure we get there before the show sells out."

"No problem, I'll be ready. That gives me just enough time."

"Just enough time?" I questioned. "You have almost three hours."

"But I want to look my best," he said.

"We're only going to a movie. It isn't like … " I paused. "Steve, who else is going to the movies tonight?"

He smiled. "I think Kim mentioned something about maybe going to the show, too. See you at eight."

# *CHAPTER THREE*

"ARE N'T YOU GOING to get changed?" my mother asked.

"What's wrong with what I'm wearing?" I asked.

"Nothing was wrong with it ... when you wore it yesterday."

"It *is* my favourite shirt."

"It would be *my* favourite shirt if it got washed. Change your clothes, put on a little deodorant, and can't you do something with your hair?"

"I can do lots of things with it," I said, and then paused. "That is, if I want."

"How about if I give you a choice?" my mother said.

"What sort of choice?"

"Either you come and finish cleaning up the kitchen, or you go and start cleaning up yourself. Well?"

"I hate the kitchen."

I started to take off my shirt as I walked away. I pulled it off over my head, balled it up, and tossed it into the laundry room. I went upstairs to the kids' bathroom. Almost the entire counter was completely filled with my sister Christina's junk. She had every product imaginable for her face and hair. If I'd spent half the time on my jump shot that she spent on her hair I'd be on my way to the NBA.

The phone rang.

"I'll get it!" Christina yelled out.

That was fine with me. Odds were that it was for her anyway—one of her many ditzy high school friends. There were times when she had calls on her cellphone and the house phone at the same time.

I put the plug into the sink and started running the water to wash up. I took the bar of soap and rubbed it between my hands, building up a lather.

"It's for you," she said as she appeared in the bathroom doorway holding the cordless phone in one hand.

"Tell whoever it is that I'll call him back after I finish washing up."

My sister gave me one of her looks—the look that said *you are beneath contempt.* "First off, I'm not here to take orders from you, and second, *he* is a girl."

"A girl?" I suddenly had the irrational urge to cover myself up. "Who is it?"

"I didn't get around to asking for a name, but I figure she's just like those other girls who call here."

"What do you mean?" I asked.

"Well, obviously anybody who calls you has to be desperate or blind or ugly."

I nodded my head. "But why would one of your friends be calling me?"

"It isn't one of my friends, it's ... oh, very funny," Christina said as she dropped the phone onto the counter beside me. She started to walk away and then spun back around. "And try to be polite," she said.

"Why wouldn't I be polite?"

"I don't know why you wouldn't be, but you never are when you talk to girls on the phone."

"Whatever," I snapped as she turned back around and walked away.

I picked up the phone. "Yeah … I mean, hello?"

"This is Denyse … you know, from basketball?"

"Yeah … what do you … how are you?"

"I'm fine. I was just calling because of the offer your mother made to drive me and Bridget to the movies. Do you think she could pick us up?"

"I guess she could. We're leaving in about ten minutes. Will you be ready?"

"We'll be ready. We'll be waiting outside on the driveway."

"Sure … okay … bye."

I put the phone down and picked up the bar of soap again. Maybe I'd better scrub a little bit harder, and where was that deodorant, and the aftershave?

"HURRY UP!" my mother called up the stairs.

"I'm coming!" I screamed back as I pulled on my shirt.

"It's just if we don't leave now we'll be late and … wow, you really did change clothes, and your hair looks nice."

"You sound surprised," I said as I did up the last of the buttons.

"Not surprised. Pleased. You look very handsome."

"That's just what every boy wants to hear ... from his *mother*," my sister said as she walked through the kitchen. "Who was that on the phone, anyway?"

"Her name is Denyse." I turned to my mother. "And she wants us to pick up her and her friend."

"You're going on a date to the movies with this girl?" my sister asked.

"No, it's not a date," I snapped. "We're just going to the same place, and Mom offered to drive. That's still okay, isn't it, Mom?"

"Of course, but why didn't you tell me we were picking her up?"

"She just called and I was getting ready. Besides, I didn't think you'd need to know until we got out to the car. And you'll drive them home, too?"

"Of course, but we'd really better get going or you're not going to get tickets to the movie."

She started out the door. I grabbed my shoes and began to lace them up. The phone rang.

"I'll get it!" Christina called out.

I tied up the first shoe.

"It's for you!" Christina yelled. "It's Steve!"

"Tell him to keep his shorts on and we'll be there in a couple of minutes!" I yelled back. I ran out the door, down the path, across the drive-way, and jumped into the front passenger seat. "Let's go!"

She backed the car out of the drive and we started away. I put down the visor and flipped open the little mirror. There was no food around my mouth. My hair looked fine and—

"You look very handsome," my mother said.

"You mentioned that."

"I just thought you might need to hear it again. So, we're picking up Denyse and a friend ... a boy or a girl?"

"Girl. At least I hope it's a girl, since her name is Bridget," I joked.

"Do you know her? Does she go to your school?"

"No, and I don't know. She might go to our school, but we all pretty much keep to our own."

"What do you mean, you keep to your own?" my mother snapped, turning to glare at me.

"Our own grade," I said, a bit confused by her response. "You know, grade eights hang around with grade eights, so if she's in grade seven, like Denyse, I wouldn't know her."

"Oh ... okay ... fine ... I understand."

"Good ... what did you think I meant?" I asked.

She didn't answer right away. "Nothing. It's silly. I just thought that you meant that ... if she was black like Denyse ... that you only hung around with—"

"White kids?" I asked.

She nodded her head.

"How could you even think something like that?" I demanded, feeling offended. "You know my friends, and you know that sort of stuff means nothing to me."

"Of course I do," she said. "And I was wrong to think that even for a split second. I'm sorry."

We came up to Denyse's house. There was still a basketball game in progress, but now there were only four people playing, one of them Denyse's brother Jamar. Denyse and another girl—I guessed it was Bridget—were standing on the grass watching the game. I recognized her. She *did* go to our school.

"I think Steve is going to be very happy about this," my mother said.

I instantly knew what she meant. Bridget was exactly the type of girl Steve was always falling in love with. She was tall and blond, and even though I couldn't see her eyes I would have bet money that they were as blue as mine.

We came to a stop in front of the driveway just as Jamar went up and did a reverse jam, slamming the ball through the hoop with such force that the whole pole shook violently.

"Wow," I gasped.

"That was quite the shot," my mother agreed.

Denyse and Bridget ran down the driveway. They opened the back door and climbed in.

"Hello, girls," my mother sang out.

"Hello, Mrs. Martin," Denyse said. "This is my friend Bridget."

"Pleased to meet you, Bridget," she said. "And do you know Thomas?"

"Sure," she answered. "At least, I've seen him around school."

"Do up your seatbelts, girls, we've really got to boogie."

"Boogie?" Bridget asked with a hint of a giggle.

I turned around in my seat. "It means 'hurry' in old people language."

The girls both burst into laughter as we started on our way.

"That was quite a shot your brother made," my mother said. "That sort of spinny, turn-around smashing shot."

"The reverse dunk," I translated.

"That's his favourite," she said. "He likes it because it looks good."

"It does look good," my mother agreed. "How come nobody on your team ever does that?" my mother asked me.

"Nobody does it because nobody *can* do it," I answered.

"Is it hard?" she asked.

"Not if you're six-five," Denyse answered.

"There must be more than just height involved," my mother said.

"Not much more. Height is all he's got. My brother has a great shot ... from less than two feet. Any-where outside of the paint and he's pretty pathetic."

"Really?" Bridget asked.

"Really. He won't even play me in twenty-one any more because he got tired of losing," Denyse said.

"You can beat him in twenty-one?" I asked in shock.

"It's no big deal," she said. "You could beat him too."

"Maybe you could play him sometime," my mother suggested.

"Me?"

"Sure. What do you think, Denyse? Do you think your brother would let Thomas play with him?"

Oh, this was getting really humiliating. Now my mother was trying to set up play-dates for me.

"Maybe. He should come over sometime and ask."

Mercifully we came up to Steve's house. I jumped out almost before the car had even come to a full stop. I ran up the path and pounded on the door. Steve appeared.

"Come on, let's get going."

"I can't go," he said.

"What? Why can't you go?"

"I'm grounded. My mother got a call from Mr. Mack about me not handing in that music assignment. That's why I called, but your sister said you were running out the door and—"

"But what am I supposed to do?" I demanded.

Steve shrugged. "Go to the movies. You're not grounded."

"But I can't go without you."

"It's not like you're by yourself. Your sister said you were going to drive Denyse. Besides, there'll be lots of other people at the theatre and, hey, who's that in the van?"

"Her name is Bridget. She's in—"

"Grade seven. I know. I've seen her around. Her locker is down at the end of the hall right beside the art room. Now I'm even more ticked off about not being able to go!"

"*You're* ticked off? How about me?"

"You get to go to the movies with them, so why are you mad?"

"I don't want to go to the movies with *them*, I want to go with you!"

"Stop whining."

"I'm not whining," I argued. "Couldn't you ask your mother if you could go out tonight and then be grounded tomorrow night?"

"Already got that covered. I'm grounded tomorrow night too ... the whole weekend. Besides, even if she said I could go out now I wouldn't have time to fix my hair ... say, your hair is looking pretty sharp."

"Thanks," I mumbled.

"I really wish I could go with you but—"

"Steven!" his mother yelled from somewhere inside the house.

"I'd better go before I'm grounded for a month. Have fun, and don't do anything I wouldn't do."

He closed the door and I just stood there, too stunned to move, staring at the door. I finally turned around, then stumbled down the stairs and along the path to the car. I opened the door and plopped down in the seat.

"Isn't he ready yet?" my mother asked. "That boy spends more time on his hair than your sister—and I didn't think that was even possible."

"He's not coming," I said. "He's grounded."

"Grounded! What did he do?"

"It's what he *didn't* do," I said. "He didn't hand in an assignment at school."

"Does that mean you're not driving us to the movies?" Bridget asked.

"Of course I'm driving you. I still have three people who want to see the movie, don't I?"

"Yeah, I want to see it," Bridget replied.

"Me too!" Denyse agreed.

I didn't say anything. I did want to see the movie, but not without Steve, or at least somebody else who was a friend.

"Thomas?" my mother asked. "Don't you want to see the movie any more?"

I didn't answer right away. "I guess I do, but I don't want to go by myself."

"You aren't going by yourself," my mother said. "You're going with these two young ladies. You three are going to stick together, aren't you?"

"Sure ... I guess we could ... I guess," Bridget said. She certainly didn't sound very enthusiastic about the idea ... but then again I wasn't so crazy about it either.

"I don't like anybody to be out by themselves," my mother continued. "It just isn't safe."

"Come on, Mom, it isn't like we'll be on a deserted island. We're going to a big theatre with hundreds and hundreds of people."

"That's the part that worries me. Those people are hundreds and hundreds of strangers, and who knows what sort of people they might be? I need the three of you to stay together."

"Mom!"

"Besides, I have to pick you all up at the end of the night so I need to have you together. Promise?"

"No problem, Mrs. Martin," Denyse said.

"Good, then let's get going."

My mother began to drive, but nobody spoke. We drove along in silence. Even my mother didn't seem to have anything to say. I kept staring straight ahead out the windshield. I could almost feel the two girls in the rear seat looking at the back of my head. They were probably wondering what they'd gotten themselves into. Heck, I was wondering what I'd gotten myself into, too, and how I could get out of it.

Before long the movie theatre appeared up ahead. There were big spotlights playing in the sky. It was a gigantic multiplex with twenty-four screens and a giant lobby with a whole bunch of little fast food places. We edged through traffic and pulled up to the curb. There was a large crowd milling around on the sidewalk out front.

"How about if we meet right here?" my mother said.

"Sounds good," I agreed.

"Thanks for the ride, Mrs. Martin," Denyse said.

"Yeah, thanks," Bridget echoed as they climbed out the back door.

"Thanks, Mom. See you around eleven-fifteen."

"Now don't forget, you're sticking together, right?"

I shot her a look that I hoped said it all, then slammed the door closed and watched as my mother pulled away from the curb and inched along in the traffic. There was a regular little traffic jam right in front. I was always amazed at how busy this place was. Didn't anybody have anything better to do on a Friday night than see a movie?

"Okay, everybody, give me your hands," Bridget said.

"What?" Denyse questioned.

"Your hands. Come on, give me your hands so that we can all stay together and nobody wanders off."

"Funny," I said.

"Let's just get inside and get our tickets," Denyse suggested.

We filtered our way through the crowd of people—mainly teenagers—who were either standing around in little bunches or wandering around. I held my breath as we passed by a group of smokers. None of them could have been any older than twelve. *Idiots*, I thought.

"What a bunch of little idiots," Denyse said, like she was reading my mind.

"Don't be so hard on them," Bridget said. "They're probably just going throcugh a phase. You must have tried a cigarette when you were younger."

"Never," Denyse said.

"Never? Not even once?"

"Not even a puff."

"Come on, don't lie," Bridget pressed.

"I'm not lying."

"Every kid experiments with smoking at least once, right, Tom?"

I shook my head. "I've never had a drag from a cigarette either."

"You two can't be for real."

"Why would anybody want to do anything as stupid as smoking?" I asked.

"That's exactly how I feel about it!" Denyse exclaimed. "Can you imagine anything more stupid than putting something in your mouth that causes cancer?"

"Something you pay a lot of money for that causes cancer," I added.

"And gives you bad breath, and yellow teeth—"

"So attractive," I said, cutting her off. "Not to mention how it hurts your lung capacity."

"Lung capacity?" Bridget asked. "What does that even mean?"

"It's the amount of air you can take into your lungs," Denyse answered.

"Oh, now *that's* important," Bridget said in a mocking tone.

"It is if you play sports," I said.

"Especially in the fourth quarter of a game," Denyse said.

"Then lung capacity can be the difference between winning—"

"And losing," Denyse said.

"This is getting weird," Bridget said.

"What's weird about not wanting to smoke?" Denyse demanded.

"Nothing. You know I don't smoke either."

"Then what's so weird?"

"Aside from the fact you two are probably the only two kids in the world who've never smoked, I think the weird thing is how you keep finishing each other's sentences. You remind me of an old married couple."

I felt myself suddenly starting to blush.

"Why don't you just shut up and let's get the tickets," Denyse said. I couldn't have said it any better myself.

Stretching out before us were more than a dozen ticket windows, with a lineup in front of each one. I surveyed the lines, trying to decide which one would be best. I'd read somewhere about how the lines in the middle were always the quickest.

"Let's go down to the far end," Denyse suggested.

"I think the middle would be faster," I said.

"No, it's definitely shorter at the far end ... I think."

I wasn't going to give Bridget another chance to say that Denyse and I we were always agreeing with each other. "You're wrong. I'm going to one of the lines in the middle. I *know* it'll be quicker."

"Sounds like we have a disagreement going on here," Bridget said. "Perhaps a little contest is in order. How about if we each pick a line and race?"

"How about if we make it a bit *more* interesting?" I suggested.

"What did you have in mind?" Denyse asked.

"How about a little bet? Last one to get a ticket has to buy popcorn for the first one."

"Where do we meet?" Denyse asked.

"Right over where they take the tickets to go in," I said, pointing to the gate.

"Sounds okay to me," Denyse said.

"Whatever," Bridget said.

"Good ... then let's go!" I yelled and ran toward one of the lines in the middle.

I skidded to a stop and Denyse ran past me. She took a spot at the end of the last line. I quickly counted the people in front of her. There were ... five or six, depending on whether somebody was buying tickets for only themselves or for other people in the line. There were only five people in front of me so I had a lead already and—the person at the start of her line got his tickets and took the person behind him out of the line. She was now in the lead!

"Excuse me," a man said, tapping me on the shoulder.

"What?" I asked, as I turned around.

"The line … aren't you going to move forward?"

I was so intent on looking at Denyse that I hadn't noticed that the line in front of me had moved two people forward! I jumped up into place just as another person got her ticket and left. I was only two people away from getting my ticket! The ticket person pushed through two tickets and some change and I was suddenly right up front.

"One for *The Long Way Home!*" I exclaimed.

"Student ticket?" she asked.

"Yeah, student!"

"Do you have your student identification?"

"Yes … yes, I do!" I fumbled in my pocket and pulled out my wallet, grabbing the I.D. from it. I pressed it against the glass.

She stared at it like she'd never seen one before. "That's eight dollars."

I stuffed a ten-dollar bill through the slot.

"I hope you don't mind quarters," she said.

"Quarters are fine!" I practically screamed. I scooped them up, grabbed my ticket, and raced toward the meeting spot! I couldn't see Denyse through the crowd ... had she already got her ticket? Was she going to beat me there? I rounded the corner in time to see Bridget up in front of me! She was going to get there first unless I ran faster. I doubled my speed, dodging around people and charging past her just before she got to the ticket-taker!

I stopped, turned around, and flashed her a big smile. "Looks like somebody is going to be buying me some popcorn."

"Not somebody," she said. "Denyse."

# *CHAPTER FOUR*

"SO, WAS THIS BET for a small, medium, or large popcorn?" Denyse asked.

"We didn't say, so I guess a medium would be fair," I said. "But, really, don't worry about it."

"Would you have bought me a popcorn if you'd lost?" Denyse asked.

"Of course."

"Then there's no problem. I'll keep my end of the bet."

Denyse and Bridget got into one of the refreshment lines—the one at the far end. Hadn't anybody learned anything? I got into a line in the very middle. Somehow I didn't feel right about Denyse buying me popcorn, but she was right, a bet was a bet. I'd use my money to

buy a super-gigantic Coke to go with it. I placed
my order, paid, and retreated out of the line,
with my giant drink. It was so big I almost
needed both hands to hold it. I could see Denyse
and Bridget, still waiting in the line at the end.
I chuckled to myself.

"Hi, Tom!"

I turned around. It was Kim and Sarah and a
couple of other girls from our school. I liked
Sarah. I hoped she liked me, too, but I didn't
really know for sure.

"How are you doing?" Kim asked. She wasn't
even looking at me. Instead she was scanning
the crowd. I assumed she was looking for
Steve.

"I'm fine ... and he's not here."

"Steve's not here?" she asked, her voice a
combination of surprise and disappointment.

"He's grounded."

"That's awful!" Kim exclaimed.

It wasn't exactly a national disaster, but I had
to admit I was feeling kind of the same way.

"So, who are you with?" Sarah asked.

"Um ... I'm ... I'm really not with anybody,"
I stammered.

"Then you can be with us," Sarah said, smiling.

I felt myself blush a little. "That would be great ... except ... I did sort of come with somebody else."

"But you just said—"

"No! I mean, my mom drove a couple of other people, that's all," I explained.

"Guys from school?" Kim asked.

"From school, but not guys," I said, reluctantly.

"Not guys? *Girls?*" Kim asked.

"Those *are* the only two choices," one of the other girls pointed out.

"You and Steve were coming to the movies with two girls?" Kim questioned.

"It's not like that!" I protested, answering Kim but looking at Sarah. "My mother just offered to drive them because they couldn't get a ride, and they live close to my house! You know them ... at least, you know one of them for sure ... Denyse, from your team."

"Denyse? You're here with Denyse?" Sarah did not sound happy.

"Not really *with*, just ... maybe we could all be together, you know, like one big group?"

"Well ... I guess that would be okay," Kim said. "Denyse is nice."

"Sure, whatever," Sarah agreed, although she still seemed kind of grumpy.

"Good, then it's settled," I said. "I hear this is a really good movie, sort of sad but funny, too."

Kim and Sarah exchanged a look, and I knew something was wrong.

"Did you get tickets for *The Long Way Home?*" Kim asked.

"Yeah. That's the movie we were all going to see, right?"

"That's the movie we *would* have seen if *somebody* hadn't spent so much time fixing her hair," one of the other girls said, shooting Kim a dirty look.

"It was sold out," Sarah explained, "so we're going to a different show."

"Maybe you could sneak into *The Long Way Home*," I suggested.

"That won't work," Kim said. "Because of all the people sneaking into shows they didn't buy tickets for, they've started to check."

I looked at the theatres that bordered the lobby. One of the lines was going in, and sure enough there were two attendants carefully checking people's tickets.

"I guess that's not going to work ... Hi, Denyse," Kim said.

"Hi, Kim." Denyse was holding a small pop and a gigantic tub of popcorn. It couldn't have been a medium, unless the large came with a forklift to carry it.

"You played an incredible game today," Kim said.

"Thanks. You played well too."

"Me? I didn't score a point."

"There's a lot more to the game than scoring," Denyse offered.

I had to agree, scoring wasn't everything, but I hadn't seen Kim do any of those other things, either.

"Here's your popcorn," Denyse said, handing me the tub.

"She bought you popcorn?" The way Sarah made it sound, it was as if Denyse had bought me a brand-new Ferrari.

"It was a bet," I quickly explained, as I fumbled to hold both the giant pop and the popcorn.

"We'd better be going," Kim said.

"Yes, we should." Sarah turned her back and walked away. The others said goodbye and chased after her. Why had she been so sharp?

Bridget started to giggle. "That one girl really seems to like you, Tom."

"I hope they all like me," I said. "We're friends."

"I don't think she likes you as just a friend," Bridget said.

What did that mean? "Which girl are you talking about?"

"The one that just went storming off."

"Sarah? She certainly didn't act like she liked me."

"That's where you're wrong. She acted that way *because* she likes you."

"You lost me," I said.

"No I didn't," Bridget said. "You were already lost."

"I still don't understand," I admitted. "What did she do that made you think she likes me?"

"Besides the way she stormed off, there was the look she gave Denyse."

"I didn't see any look."

"I did," Denyse said. "If looks could kill I'd be a dead girl."

"But why wouldn't she like you?"

"Isn't it obvious?"

"Not to me."

"She's mad at Denyse because she thinks she's putting the moves on you," Bridget explained.

"You're joking, right?"

"She's joking about me putting the moves on you, anyway."

"I didn't say you *were*," Bridget replied. "You never put the moves on anybody, Denyse. I'm saying that that Sarah girl *thought* you were putting the moves on Tom."

"Well, you can tell her she has nothing to worry about from me," Denyse said.

All at once I felt relieved and disappointed. Girls were so confusing. I never felt this mixed up when I went to the movies with Steve.

"We'd better get going too," Denyse said. "The movie starts in a few minutes."

Bridget shook her head. "We have plenty of time. The show doesn't start until nine-thirty-five," she said. "It's right here on the ticket."

"Let me see." Denyse took the ticket from Bridget. She looked at it closely. "You're right, Bridget, the movie you're going to see does start then."

"Like I said."

"But the movie Tom and I are going to see starts at nine-fifteen."

"What?"

Denyse handed her back her ticket. "We bought tickets to see *The Long Way Home* and you bought a ticket for *Going All the Way*."

"No way!" Bridget exclaimed.

"Let me have a look," I suggested, and Bridget handed me the ticket. There was no doubt—she had a ticket for a different show. "Sorry," I said as I handed it back to her.

"Maybe I can just go into your show," Bridget said.

"You can try, but they're checking all the tickets at the doors."

"Then maybe I could go back and tell them there's been a mistake, and they could trade this ticket for the right one."

"That won't work either," I said. "The show is sold out."

"Then what am I going to do?" Bridget pleaded.

"You're going to go to see your movie and we're going to see ours, and then we'll all meet back here when they're over," Denyse said.

"But——"

"No time to argue," Denyse said, cutting her off. "*Our* movie is about to start."

Denyse walked away and I stumbled after her. "Hold on!" I called out, and she stopped.

"Don't worry about her, she'll be okay."

"I'm not worried about that. I just need to get something to put on my popcorn."

"Okay … fine … but hurry."

"By the way, you didn't have to get me a large popcorn. The bet was for a medium."

"It was only twenty-five cents more for twice as much popcorn, and a movie's hardly a movie without popcorn," Denyse said.

"But you don't have any popcorn."

"I shouldn't have made that bet. I didn't have enough money for two."

"I'm sorry."

"Don't be. I'd be eating your popcorn if you'd lost."

"I'd offer to share——there's plenty——but I eat my popcorn with a really strange topping," I said.

Denyse laughed. "Nobody puts anything stranger on top of it than me!"

"You don't want to make that bet," I said. "I sprinkle sugar on my popcorn. What do you put on yours?"

Her eyes widened. "Sugar. I put on sugar."

"You're kidding me, right?"

She shook her head.

"I've never met anybody else who eats their popcorn that way. Most people think that it's—"

"Disgusting," Denyse said, finishing both my sentence and my thought once again.

"Yeah, disgusting."

"I like the way the sweet of the sugar and the salty of the popcorn are so different but go together so well," she said.

I put the tub of popcorn down on the counter while I grabbed some sugar packets and stuffed them in my pockets. "Exactly!"

The theatre was almost completely filled as we entered. There was a real buzz of conversation as people talked and laughed while they waited for the lights to dim and the movie to start.

"Where do you want to sit?" Denyse asked.

"I like to sit close to the back, but I don't think we have much choice. It looks like everything except for the first few rows is gone."

We walked down the aisle. I saw a lot of familiar faces and nodded and said hello to some kids that I knew. Denyse did the same to people she knew and I didn't. It seemed like a whole big chunk of our school was there in the theatre that night. We settled into our seats as the lights started to dim.

"We're just in time ... for the previews," I said.

"I don't mind the previews," Denyse said.

"Me neither. That's usually how I find out what I want to see next. What drives me crazy are the commercials."

"I hate those!" Denyse agreed. "It just seems plain wrong to have to pay money to see commercials."

"I make a point of trying never to buy anything that's been in a commercial at the movies. Of course, since most of them are for cars, beer, vodka, and gaming systems that I can't afford, it isn't that hard," I admitted.

Denyse laughed. She had a nice laugh and a great smile—the one I'd noticed from across the gym floor.

I ripped open one of the sugar packets and started to sprinkle it on the popcorn.

"Let me help," Denyse offered.

I dug into my pocket and pulled out a bunch of packets.

"You really do like sugar, don't you?" she said.

"The more the better."

We finished dumping on the sugar and tasted our creation. It was just about perfect.

There was only one commercial——for a really expensive car——and three previews before the movie started rolling. I slumped down into my seat even farther and snuggled down to make myself comfortable. I put the gigantic pop on the floor between my feet. It was way too big to fit in the drink holder on the seat. The tub of popcorn was balanced on the armrest between my seat and Denyse's.

As the opening titles flowed across the screen I found myself thinking more about the girl sitting beside me than the movie in front of me. She liked sugar on her popcorn ... that was unbelievable. I reached over to grab some popcorn and our hands touched. I felt a jolt of electricity surge through my body and I quickly pulled my hand away!

"Sorry," I mumbled.

"Me too," Denyse stammered. "Here, you take it," she said, as she pushed the tub of popcorn toward me.

"No, we're going to share it!"

"Could we all share a little silence so we can watch the movie?" a voice hissed out of the darkness behind us.

"Sorry," I said as I slumped even lower into my seat.

THE MOVIE CAME TO AN END and the credits began to roll.

"Do you mind if we stay and watch the credits?" Denyse asked.

I shrugged. "There's no point in rushing off. We might as well sit here instead of standing out there waiting for Bridget."

Line after line rolled onto the screen. After the first few names—the stars of the movie—I didn't recognize anybody. Then it got to the point where I couldn't even figure out what they did. What exactly was a key grip, anyway? The final line rolled up: "Based on the novel *Diamonds in the Rough*."

The lights came up then and the screen turned to black. Denyse and I stood and joined the end of the line exiting the theatre. We shuffled into the crowded lobby and bumped into the other half of our school as we moved toward the spot where we were to meet Bridget.

"I'm thirsty," Denyse said.

"I still have some Coke left," I offered.

Denyse leaned over and, without taking the pop from my hand, took a long sip. "Thanks."

I looked at my watch a bit anxiously. "My mother doesn't wait well."

"But we can't go anywhere without Bridget."

"I know. We'll have to hope that she isn't much longer, or my mother might figure out that we actually let her out of our sight for more than a split second. We can tell her that the movie went longer than we thought."

"Longer would have been okay with me," Denyse said.

"Me too. It was good."

"And do you know one of the things that made it good?"

"Sugar on the popcorn?" I joked.

"That too, but I was thinking that I really liked it because you were sitting beside me."

"Me?" I felt myself start to blush big time now.

"Don't get me wrong—Bridget is one of my best friends—but it was so much better to have you there instead of her. She's always asking questions and making comments ... the girl doesn't know how to be quiet. But you just sat there and watched the movie."

"It bugs me too when people jabber all through the—hey, there's Bridget!"

"Good, let's get going."

We waved to Bridget and then headed out to the street, where I was pretty sure my mother would be waiting, probably a bit impatiently, in the car. Funny, for an evening I'd kind of been dreading, I was sorry to see it end.

# CHAPTER FIVE

"COULDN'T YOU JUST drop it over?" I asked my mother.

My mother had found Denyse's purse in the back seat that morning while she was cleaning out the car. She must have forgotten it when we'd dropped her off at home after the movie.

"She's your friend, Thomas. Besides, I have to finish cleaning the kitchen ... unless you want to do it?"

"Come on, Mom, be reasonable."

"I am being reasonable."

"Can't it wait until Monday? I could give it to her at school."

"No, it can't wait. A purse is a very personal thing, and I'm sure Denyse will want it back as soon as possible."

"But there's no snow on the ground—how often does that happen in February? I just wanted to go rollerblading for a while."

"You can," my mother said.

"I can?"

"Sure. Strap on your blades and skate over to Denyse's house."

"Mom!"

"Not another word, or you'll blade over and then come back and clean the kitchen, too."

I pretended to zipper my mouth closed. My mother was pretty easygoing, but you really didn't want to cross her.

I finished the last of my breakfast and brought the dirty dishes over to the sink, then I went upstairs and threw on some clothes. Just as I was getting ready to head back downstairs I caught my reflection in the mirror in the corner of my room. There was a stain on my shirt, and my hair looked as though it had been through something sticky and a wind tunnel. The shirt I could change, although I was going to put a hoodie over top of it anyway, and the hair didn't matter because I was going to be wearing a helmet. I rummaged around in my top drawer until I found a shirt that was a nice combination of clean and cool. I changed shirts, grabbed my hoodie, and headed downstairs.

The purse was sitting on the bench right beside my blades and helmet. I slipped on the first boot and laced it up, nice and tight. I put on the second and did the same. They were a little tight in the toe. Maybe my feet had grown— I hadn't really done much blading in the past two months. Rollerblading and snow didn't go together too well. I grabbed my helmet and put it on, leaving the strap undone. Maybe it wouldn't protect me in a fall, but it was a compromise: my mother would be happy to see me wearing a helmet, and it still looked pretty cool as long as the strap was hanging down.

I stood up and did a tight little spin in the entranceway. That felt good.

"Don't forget your helmet!" my mother yelled from the kitchen.

"Got it on!" I called back.

"Tom, are you wearing a coat? It's freezing out!"

"I've got a hoodie. Be back in an hour or two!"

I picked up the purse and practically jumped out the door before she could insist on a coat over top or ask me anything more about where I was going. I was just going to skate ... go up to the plaza and grind on a curb ... maybe run into a few friends ... maybe drop into somebody's house and chill. She didn't need to know where I was every minute. And I really didn't need a coat because I'd be plenty warm enough once I got moving.

I jumped down the three stairs off the porch, landed with a thud, rolled along the path, down the driveway, and onto the street, catching some air as I left the curb. Maybe I hadn't forgotten how to skate after all. I pumped my legs to pick up some speed. It felt really good. Just about the only thing that compared to the feeling of rollerblading was snowboarding—that was how I spent my wintertime on the slopes. The two were pretty similar, and a lot of the tricks I did in one I could do in the other.

At the end of the street I came to my favourite house ... well, not really my favourite house, but my favourite wall. It was about two feet high and smooth. I loved grinding on that wall. I loved grinding it as much as the owner hated me doing it. I guess you could have called it a love/hate sort of thing.

There was a car in the driveway, so somebody was probably home, but there was nobody in the yard or looking out the front window. I pumped harder to pick up some speed, hopped over the curb and onto the sidewalk, and then jumped up onto the wall doing a variation on a sole grind, with my front foot riding the wall along the outside of the sole of the boot and my back boot riding on the grind plate. I slid along for a split second and then one of the wheels caught. I stumbled and had to jump off to stop myself from crashing. Not a great trick, but any trick you skated away from with all your teeth in place and your bodily fluids still inside your body was okay.

I jumped off the curb, caught a little air, and made a grab at one blade. Not a bad grab. Nothing fancy, but okay. I bladed off the road and onto a walking path. It cut between my street and Denyse's. I could probably blade between our two houses faster than somebody could drive a car because they'd have to follow the road and go around the big curve.

The path was deserted except for a couple of people walking their dogs. I passed a man bent over, plastic bag over his hand, picking up after his pet. That was the worst part about walking a dog ... especially if somebody was watching. It was basically impossible to look cool when you were holding a bag full of dog crap. Although blading while holding a purse tucked under my arm wasn't a whole lot better.

I skated onto Denyse's street and almost immediately saw her. She was on the driveway, her back to me, shooting baskets—foul shots. She missed the shot and the ball bounced right back to her. She bounced it, spun the ball, and put up another shot that dropped for a basket.

"Hi," I said as I came up to the driveway and circled to a stop. I hoped I looked as cool as I thought I did.

Denyse smiled in reply.

"Practising?" I asked.

She nodded. "I hate missing foul shots. I feel so stupid. Everybody's watching and there's nobody to stop you and the shot *still* doesn't drop."

"The worst for me is taking a technical shot when nobody is even on your side of the half."

"It's awful to miss those. That's why I practise foul shooting so much. I keep shooting until I make six shots in a row," she said.

"That could take a long time."

"Sometimes I can do it in ten minutes," Denyse said.

"And other times?"

She didn't answer right away. "Once it took me almost six hours."

"You're not serious, are you?"

"I made five in a row a dozen times but couldn't drop the sixth. I kept going until I finally made it. Pretty nuts, huh?"

"You're talking to the wrong guy," I said. "Did you do the charity walk at school a few weeks ago?"

"Yeah."

"So did I. I finished the whole walk."

"A bunch of people did," she said.

"I didn't stop."

"I don't think I stopped either," Denyse said.

"Did you have a pebble in your shoe for the entire walk, digging into the bottom of your right foot every time you took a step?"

She gave me a questioning look.

"It was there from almost the beginning of the walk, but I'd promised myself that I wouldn't stop ... so I didn't even stop to take it out."

"You're right," Denyse said, "you're nuts too."

"Thank you ... I think."

"By the way," she said, "nice purse."

"I guess so," I mumbled, not sure what else to say.

"Do you always carry a purse when you go rollerblading?"

"Never ... I mean, just this once. Here," I said, holding it out for Denyse.

She didn't move to take it.

"It's yours."

She shook her head. "It's not mine."

"But it was left in our car last night ... my mother said it was yours."

"Actually, it does look familiar. It's Bridget's."

"But why would my mother think that it was yours?"

"I don't know ... wait a second." Denyse took the purse, opened it, and pulled out some sort of makeup. "These are mine, so your mother would have figured it was my purse."

"But why would she think that it's yours instead of Bridget's?" I asked.

"Because of the makeup."

"Does it have your name on it?" I asked.

She laughed. "No. It's because Bridget is white and I'm black."

"I, um ... noticed that, but I still don't understand," I said.

"You don't know much about makeup, do you?" Denyse said.

"Nothing at all," I readily admitted. "You know, the guys and I, we don't spend a whole lot of time chatting about it. We're funny that way."

"Well, people with different skin tones use different shades of foundation. This matches my skin," she explained.

"I didn't even know you wore makeup," I said, struggling for something to say that might be on topic.

"I don't wear much. I can't get over girls who show up to play basketball looking like they're going out to a party."

"That's never a problem with the guys."

She laughed politely.

"Maybe I should let you go back to taking your shots."

"That's okay. Those are pretty fancy blades you're wearing, by the way."

"Pretty expensive, too, but aggressive inline blades like these are a lot different from the regular blades."

"How are they different?" Denyse asked.

"For starters, they don't have brakes."

"Yeah, but don't you kind of need the brakes to stop—you know, like when you're heading straight for a brick wall or something?"

"You can stop, it's just a little harder. The boots are also made of tougher stuff. The carriage—the place where the wheels attach—is stronger, and there's a grind plate in the middle of the wheels … right here," I said, holding up one skate and pointing to the plate.

"So those blades are made for doing tricks, right?" Denyse asked.

"That's right."

"Can you do any tricks?"

"I can do plenty of tricks … grabs, grinds, jumps, spins."

"I saw a video on TV with guys wearing blades like that and they were sliding along rails and down stairs."

"I can do that stuff."

"And there was this one guy who actually jumped off the roof of a garage," she continued.

"I could do that, too," I said. "Well ... at least I could do it once. Then I'd have to wait about three or four months for all the bones to heal before I did it a second time."

Denyse laughed and flashed me that smile again—that beautiful smile. "Could you show me a couple of tricks?"

"I ... I guess I could." I looked around. I really couldn't see any place to grind, and the only way to catch air would be by jumping off the curb. Not particularly exciting to watch. Across the street the driveways sloped down from the houses to the road. If I skated down one of those I could pick up enough speed that even a little jump off the curb might give me enough air to do a grab.

"Maybe I can do something," I said.

I skated down her driveway, onto the road, and up the other driveway. I did a spin turn at the top and came straight down the driveway, pumping my legs fast enough to gain speed for—

"Look out!" Denyse screamed.

# *CHAPTER SIX*

I SKIDDED ACROSS THE ASPHALT, face first, my helmet sliding along across the road, and I got to the other side just before the car passed.

"Didn't you see that car?" Denyse screamed as she raced toward me.

I'd been focusing so much on the trick that I hadn't even noticed it. Now the sharp pain in my side let me know I wasn't okay ... it was just a question of how not-okay. I pushed myself up with my hands ... the left one was scraped up. I got to my feet just as Denyse reached my side.

"Are you all right?"

The knee was ripped out of my pants and blood was staining the material.

"Your pants are ripped ... you're bleeding!" Denyse exclaimed.

"My mom is going to kill me. She hates it when I ruin my clothes."

"But what about the blood ... the injury ... you're hurt!"

"Not bad. Whatever it is will heal." I paused. "It does sting, though." I lifted my leg and almost lost my balance. Denyse grabbed onto me and stopped me from tumbling over.

"I ... I feel a little dizzy," I stammered.

"You banged your head."

"Maybe just a little."

"Hard enough to make it bleed," Denyse said.

"Bleed ... where?" I reached up and my hand came away with the answer to my question—it was stained with blood.

"If you'd had your helmet done up your head would have been okay," Denyse scolded me.

"Now you sound like my mother ... boy, is she going to get mad about my head being cut up ... even more than the pants being ruined."

"Come on," Denyse said as she started to walk back toward her house. She stopped and turned around. "Are you coming?"

Slowly, carefully, I started to blade. As I passed my helmet I bent over and scooped it up. I turned it over in my hands—at least *it* wasn't hurt. I followed Denyse up her driveway and stopped at the bottom of the stairs leading to her porch. I sat down on the bottom step.

"Can't you get up the stairs?" Denyse asked.

"Of course I can."

"Then come on up. You don't expect me to fix you up out on the driveway, do you?"

I hadn't really expected her to fix anything, anywhere, but it would be good not to have to go home bleeding. Slowly, on wobbly legs, I climbed the stairs and moved across the porch. Denyse was holding the front door to her house open and motioned me inside.

"Take your blades off," she said.

I sat down on a deacon's bench just inside the door and quickly took off my blades, putting them beside the door. Denyse disappeared down the hall. Was I supposed to wait or follow after her? Tentatively I padded down the hall and peeked into a room. It was the kitchen, but she was nowhere to be seen. What should I do now?

A moment later Denyse walked into the kitchen from the other direction. She was carrying a big white box.

"Have a seat," she said, pointing to the kitchen table.

I pulled out a chair and sat down. She plopped the box down on the table with a thud and unsnapped its latches. When she opened it up I could see it was full of bandages and splints and gauze and ointments. It was a gigantic first-aid kit!

"Do you want a Coke?" she asked.

"Definitely."

"With lots of ice, right?"

"Yeah ... how did you know?"

"Just figured. That's how I like mine." She took two glasses from the cupboard and an ice tray out of the freezer. She emptied the tray into the two glasses and then poured the Coke from a big bottle. The pop fizzed and foamed up to the top. I could smell it. She handed me the glass and I took a long sip. Nothing like a glass of Coke in the morning. That combination of caffeine and sugar could really get your engine started.

"That's quite the first-aid kit," I said.

"Believe me, around here we need it. There's hardly a game on the driveway that doesn't end up with somebody being hurt in some way."

"A lot of ball gets played out there," I commented, thinking about all the games I'd witnessed as I walked by over the years.

"A whole lot, and the general rule is: no blood, no foul. Things can get pretty rough, especially when my brothers are playing against each other. I'm surprised somebody hasn't gotten killed. Of course, that doesn't happen so often now that two of them have gone away to university."

"They're on basketball scholarships, right?" I asked.

"My big brother is on a basketball scholarship, but not the next one."

"He doesn't play basketball?"

"He plays for the university team, but he's not on a basketball scholarship. He's in school on an *academic* scholarship. His marks are amazing." She paused. "I heard your marks are pretty good, too."

"How did you hear that?"

"From Bridget. She knows everything about everybody."

I laughed. "Steve is like that, too."

"So, are your marks as good as Bridget said?"

"They're okay," I said. My lowest mark was a 92, but I didn't like people to know that. Some people figured if you were smart you had to be some sort of geek who couldn't play sports.

"Let's start with the leg," Denyse said. "Roll up your pants."

I pulled up the cuff and revealed a large, nasty scrape. Denyse put on a pair of latex gloves. She took a cotton ball, opened up a bottle, and dabbed the cotton ball against it.

"This is going to sting a bit," she warned.

"Not as much as the fall did."

Gently, she placed the cotton ball against the cut and I gritted my teeth as a searing pain shot up my leg. It faded to a burning sensation as she continued to dab away at the blood, revealing the gash underneath. It didn't look that big ... at least, compared to some others I'd got blading.

"Hold this," Denyse said as she placed a piece of gauze against the cut. She then took two strips of tape and secured it in place.

"You're pretty good at this," I said.

"Lots of practice."

"You'd make a good doctor."

"As it happens, I'm thinking about a career in medicine. My marks aren't too shabby either. Now let's look at your head."

"Don't worry, it's okay."

"Don't argue with the doctor." Denyse walked over to the counter and took a cloth, turned on the tap, and ran it under the water. She wrung out the cloth and brought it back over.

"Lower your head."

She took the cloth and rubbed it against my scalp. It hurt, but I didn't say a word.

"It doesn't look too bad," she said. "Scalps bleed easily. Best to put some ice on it." She went back to the sink and rinsed out the cloth under the tap again, and red drained into the sink. She then took another tray of ice out of the refrigerator and dropped some of the cubes into the cloth. She wrapped it up and then walked over and pressed it against the side of my head.

"You know, when I was little I wanted to have hair like yours," Denyse said.

"You wanted to have blond hair?"

"I wanted to have *white* hair."

"But my hair isn't white. It's sort of dirty blond, or ..." I stopped myself as I suddenly realized what she meant.

"Don't get me wrong," she said. "I like my hair *now*, but when I was little I didn't. Blame it on Barbie."

"Barbie who?"

"Barbie the doll. She had so much great stuff, and she always seemed to be having so much fun that I wanted to at least have hair like hers."

"But isn't there a black Barbie? Well, not Barbie, but a friend of Barbie's ... right?"

"Yeah, but she's not important. She's more like the token doll to show that Barbie isn't a racist or anything. Besides, I didn't want to *be* white, I just wanted white hair."

"It's probably just human nature to want what you don't have," I said.

"Probably. Did you ever want to have black hair?"

"Umm ... not really ... although I think it would be kind of cool to have no hair, you know, shave my head, but when white guys do it they always look goofy."

"I think black or white they look goofy."

"And I really like your hair now," I offered. It was all braided in tight little plaits.

"Do you really? Thanks." She paused. "But still, it is different. Here, feel my hair."

I hesitated.

"Here," she said as she reached over and grabbed my hand, bringing it up to her head. It felt strange—not so much the hair as having my hand against a girl's head, touching her head.

"Feel the difference?" she said.

"It is different, I guess ... but good ... and it smells good."

"Thanks, I've been using this new shampoo and—"

"What the hell is going on here?" yelled out a voice.

I dropped my hand from Denyse's hair, jumped to my feet, and spun around. It was Denyse's brother Jamar. He stood in the doorway, taking up most of it, with a scowl plastered on his face.

"This is my friend Thomas, from school."

"I didn't ask who he is or where he's from, I want to know what's going on!" He sounded really angry.

"Thomas got hurt. I was only taking care of his cuts."

"And just how was his hand on your head taking care of any cuts? It looked like he was petting you like you were a dog!"

Denyse stood up and stomped across the kitchen until she was standing toe to toe with her brother. He towered over her. "I don't have to explain anything to you!" she snapped.

"You're right," Jamar said, "you don't have to explain anything."

I felt a sudden sense of relief.

"But," Jamar said as he stepped around his sister and came toward me, "this *boy* had better start explaining things to me, or he's gonna have a few more cuts that need to be treated!"

I felt a rush of fear and had to fight the urge to run out of the room.

"Your coach isn't gonna like you beating up on another Monarch player!" Denyse snapped.

Jamar skidded to a stop and spun around. "What do you mean?"

"He plays for the Monarchs."

He spun back around and poked a finger in my face. "You play for the Monarchs?"

I nodded my head vigorously up and down. "Yeah … Bantam … triple A team."

He looked me up and down like he was sizing me up, to see if I looked more like a basketball player or a liar.

"This is my third year playing rep."

He nodded his head and his expression softened ever so slightly. "So what are you doing here?"

"It's like I told you. He got hurt. I was fixing him up. He was over here dropping off something I left in his car last night."

"Car?" Jamar exclaimed. "You have a car?"

"No, of course not—it's my mother's car!" I protested. "She was driving us back from the movies and—"

"You two went to the movies together?" Jamar's expression was now even harder than before.

"Not together … just at the same time … like friends!"

His expression softened again. "Well … I guess that's okay."

"Friends who sat side by side and shared popcorn and who drove to and from the movie together," Denyse said.

Why was she saying these things? Was she actually trying to make him angry?

"But just as *friends*," I said, emphasizing the last word as much as I could.

"Good," Jamar said. "Good."

"Is it?" Denyse walked over and stepped between Jamar and me. It felt good to have a little more distance from him. She then reached up and pointed a finger right into his face. "I'm so *happy* that you approve," she said, "because your approval means so much to me!" The sarcasm was practically dripping from her voice. "Because I want you to know that if Thomas and I were more than friends it would be absolutely no business of yours. I am not your *daughter*. I am your *sister*. So, do you understand?"

Jamar smiled and his whole body posture seemed to relax. "You're right, Denyse. You are not my daughter ... you are my sister ... my little twelve-year-old sister, and nobody better *mess with her*." He said the last three words slow and low and staring me right in the eyes.

# CHAPTER SEVEN

"SO HOW'S IT GOING, lover boy?" Steve asked as he walked up to me in the hall.

"Lover boy?" I questioned. "I really think you've misunderstood how I feel about you, Steve. I *like* you, but I think of you as just a *friend*."

For a few seconds Steve looked confused, then, "Funny, very funny," he said. "I was talking about Denyse, you idiot!"

It was my turn to look confused.

"Don't go acting dumb on me. I know all about the movie."

"No, not *all* about it. You would have known *all* about it if you hadn't been grounded," I said.

"I still know plenty."

"What's there to know? Denyse and I went to the same movie. But you knew that on Friday when you couldn't go."

"Yes, but it's what I found out this morning that interests me. Like the fact that the two of you ditched Bridget and—"

"We did *not* ditch Bridget. She bought a ticket to the wrong movie!" I protested. "There was nothing we could do about it!"

"No? How about if you and Bridget had traded tickets? Then you could have seen a movie by yourself and the two girls could have been together," Steve suggested.

"Umm ... I really hadn't thought about that."

"Hadn't thought about it, or didn't want to think about it?" Steve asked. "I also heard that you and Denyse shared popcorn, and she was taking sips from your pop."

"A sip ... *one* sip ... not *sips*."

"That's still sharing some saliva."

"Don't be disgusting!"

Steve chuckled. "And I heard that you went over to her house the next day."

"That was because she forgot her purse in my car."

"Bridget's purse. You brought Bridget's purse to Denyse's house."

"I thought it was Denyse's!" I exclaimed.

"That's what you *wanted* to think so you could see her again," Steve said.

"Wait a minute. Who's been telling you all this stuff?" I demanded.

"I have lots of sources. It sounds like I was the only person in the whole school who wasn't at Silver City on Friday."

"I guess everybody else in the school handed in their assignments," I said.

"Don't rub it in. So when are you going to see Denyse again?"

"I'm not."

"She dumped you already?"

"She didn't dump me!"

"Good, because I was hoping that maybe you and me and Denyse and Bridget could go to a movie this—"

The two-minute warning bell rang, drowning out the last part of Steve's sentence.

"The only place I'm planning on going is to class. And if you're half smart—and sometimes I wonder about that—you'll get to class too or you'll be late, in trouble, grounded again, and going nowhere this weekend either."

I THREADED MY WAY across the cafeteria, balancing my tray in one hand and my books and a drink in the other. I was heading to my usual spot in the back corner when I caught sight of Denyse. She was sitting at a table with a bunch of other grade sevens, including Bridget. Denyse saw me looking at her and smiled and gave a little wave. I nodded back.

"Tommy!" Bridget screamed and waved her arms above her head like she was trying to flag a taxi. Everybody who wasn't staring at her seemed to be staring at me. I altered my course and moved toward them.

"How you doing?" I asked.

"Good. You?"

"Okay for a Monday," I replied.

"Has anybody been bothering you this morning?" Denyse asked.

"Bothering me?" I asked.

"Yeah, you know, asking you stupid questions?"

"Oh," I said, nodding my head. "You mean like gossiping."

"Exactly."

"I guess some people lead such pathetic lives themselves that they have no choice but to gossip about other people," I said.

"I resent that remark," Bridget said.

"No, girl," Denyse said, "you *resemble* that remark."

All the other girls at the table began to snicker.

"I'm just being a good friend," Bridget protested. "A good friend who's showing a friendly concern for my friend Denyse's life."

"Is that what you call it?" I asked. "Then I guess Steve is just really genuinely concerned about my life, too."

"He's cute," Bridget said. "Do you think he might ever show a little friendly concern about my life?"

"Bridget!" Denyse exclaimed.

"What? There's no harm in letting him know that I might like him." She turned to me. "You'll let him know, won't you?"

"What do I look like, the mailman?"

"Do you want to join us for lunch?" Denyse asked.

"I should probably eat with my friends," I replied. "Besides, isn't there enough talk already?"

"You're probably right," she agreed.

"That's strange," Bridget said.

"What's strange?" Denyse asked.

"I just didn't think either of you two would care what people say. I figured you'd do what you wanted to do."

Denyse and I exchanged a look. She pushed out a chair and I sat down beside her.


"THOMAS!" my mother yelled up the stairs. "Pick up the telephone, your dad is on the line!"

I dropped my book, jumped off the bed, and picked up the extension.

"How you doing, Dad?"

"I'm doing well, really well!" he said. He certainly sounded happy.

"I'm going to hang up now," my mother said. "I'll leave you two to talk. And I'll see you Friday, honey."

"See you then. Love you," my father said.

"Me too ... be safe," my mother replied, and then she hung up the phone.

"Friday?" I asked my dad. "I thought you weren't coming back until sometime next week."

"Business wrapped up early. So, how are things going for you?" he asked.

"Pretty good."

"School?"

"Good, as always," I replied.

"How about basketball?" My father loved basketball, so I was surprised he'd even asked about school.

"The school team is doing okay, and the rep team even better."

"Your mom also mentioned a girl."

"A girl? What girl?" I asked.

"Are there so many that you don't know which one I'm talking about?"

"No, of course not!"

He laughed. "I think your mother said her name is Denyse."

"She's just a friend."

"Well, that's how a lot of the best relationships start out."

"Dad!"

"Nothing to be embarrassed about," he said.

"I'm not embarrassed!" I protested, even though I was.

"When I was your age——"

"The wheel hadn't been invented yet," I said, cutting him off. I needed to change the subject. "So, if you're back on Friday, can we go skiing on Saturday?"

"I promised you we'd go as soon as I got back, and a promise is a promise."

"Great!"

"And if you want to bring along a friend or two, that's okay. There's lots of extra seats in the van, and we have a bunch of guest passes for the club."

"Great. I'll invite somebody."

"Okay. And Tom, when I said a friend, that could be a guy *or* a girl, you know."

"Dad!"

"I was just saying ..."

I COULDN'T SLEEP. I lay on the bed and tried to read, but my mind kept drifting back to the conversation with my father. It wasn't that unusual a topic. He often brought up girls and dating and stuff like that. But it wasn't the sort of thing I was comfortable talking about to anybody, and certainly not my father. Thank goodness it was one topic that my mother avoided, though, because that would have been much, much worse.

I was thinking that I could invite Steve to go skiing with me. My father skied and Steve and I both boarded, so we could hang out together in the terrain park. My father had said I could invite more than one person ... I wondered if Denyse even skied, and if she did, would she want to come with us? No, that was crazy! I'd go with my father and Steve. There, that was settled. I'd ask Steve tomorrow. Nothing left to think about.

So why was I still having trouble getting to sleep?

# *CHAPTER EIGHT*

"THIS HAS GOT TO BE the best way in the world to end the week," Steve said as we shuffled forward in the line leading into the gym. "Why don't they do this every Friday instead of once a month?"

"Probably because the teachers have this crazy idea that learning math and science is more important than a school dance," I said.

"You're right ... that *is* crazy. Nothing that happened in school this week is as important or as educational as what's about to happen in here during the next three periods."

"Dances are okay," I said.

"You might think they were more than just okay if you actually tried dancing."

"I dance!"

"No, what you do is stand by the wall waiting for somebody to ask you to dance, and that doesn't happen too often."

"It happens."

"You know, it's okay for you to ask people to dance."

"I've asked."

"When?" Steve demanded.

I didn't answer. It was probably two years ago when I was in grade six.

"Then again," Steve said, "maybe it's better if you don't dance at all."

"How do you figure that?"

"First time I saw you up on the dance floor thrashing around I almost ran to call for an ambulance, because I thought you were having a seizure."

"Thanks for the confidence booster ... that really makes me want to get out there on the dance floor."

"I'm just kidding. You dance okay ... for a white guy."

We got to the front of the line and handed over the tickets we'd bought—fifty cents each, with the proceeds going to the library. We headed into the gym. Most of the lights were turned off and it was difficult to see. I figured that was a good thing. Nobody would have had the nerve to dance under the bright lights. I wasn't the only one who looked like he was having a seizure when he danced.

I followed behind Steve as he worked his way through the crowded gym. It was packed. Almost the entire school was crammed in there. But that was no surprise—the choice was either to fork over the fifty cents and go to the dance or stay in class and work.

The dance floor was at the very front, by the big speakers set up on the stage, and it was the only space in the whole gym that wasn't crowded. Three girls were dancing together there, and one brave couple. I wondered if I looked as stupid as they did when I danced.

Steve reached the edge of the dance floor and turned to the left—that was different, we usually went over to the right to hold up a piece of that wall. We tiptoed around the floor as if we were afraid we might burn our feet if we got too far onto it.

Steve stopped and turned around. "There they are."

"Who?"

"Bridget and Denyse. I'm going to ask Bridget to dance."

"But what about Kim?" I asked.

"Kim is so *last* week," Steve explained, without a hint of sarcasm. "Besides, I'm doing this for you."

"Me?"

"Of course. Last week I was going after Kim because I thought you liked her best friend, Sarah … even though I didn't think you and Sarah were right together."

"You didn't?"

"Nah," he said, shaking his head. "You two have nothing in common. Not like you and Denyse."

Instinctively I was going to argue, but he was right. We did seem to have a lot in common. Besides, Sarah always seemed sort of snooty, with fancy hair, and what was with those nails? How could anybody even pick up a pen when their nails were all long and fancy like that? I couldn't even imagine her playing basketball.

"And now that you like Denyse, I'm being friendly with Bridget."

"So that's why you're doing it? Gee, thanks."

"You *should* be thanking me. Consider the *sacrifices* I make for you," Steve explained.

"Wait until I tell Bridget that she's a sacrifice you're making for me."

"You wouldn't!" he exclaimed, sounding worried.

"Don't tempt me or I might." I walked past Steve toward the girls. We yelled "hellos" over the music, which seemed to have just gotten louder by a few decibels. Steve leaned close to Bridget and said something to her. She nodded, and the two of them headed off to the dance floor.

"I think they like each other!" Denyse yelled into my ear.

"Steve's always willing to make a sacrifice," I replied.

"What?"

"Oh, nothing."

We stood side by side, not talking, staring at the dance floor, which had now started to fill up. It was always interesting to watch how, after the first few couples got on the floor and others saw that they hadn't been struck by lightning, it quickly became crowded.

"You dance?" Denyse asked.

"Not very well," I admitted.

"Me neither."

I knew what question was supposed to come next—"Do you want to dance?"—but somehow I couldn't get the words to squeeze out of my head and into my mouth.

"Do you want to dance?" Denyse asked.

I felt a sense of relief that she'd been the one to ask the question, and also anxiety that either of us had asked the question at all.

"Um … I guess … but could we wait until something different comes on? I really don't know how to dance to rap."

"I don't think anybody can dance to rap, it's just that some people are smart enough to realize it," she said. "I don't even like listening to it."

"You don't? I thought you'd like rap."

"Why?" Denyse asked. "Because I'm black?"

"No, of course not," I said, although that did kind of make sense to me. "I just thought that everybody liked rap."

"Not me. And the only thing worse than the music is the videos that go along with them."

"I like some of the videos," I said.

"What's to like?" Denyse demanded. "A bunch of thugs and losers who can't sing, mouthing off about treating women badly, doing drugs, and hurting people. To top it off, they have enough jewellery around their necks to anchor a boat, and everybody has big, baggy pants hanging halfway off their ... their bottoms."

I was wearing a pair of pants so big on me that if I hadn't been wearing a belt they would have been around my knees.

The rap song came to an end—thank God— and a slow song came on.

"At least this one I know how to dance to," Denyse said.

She grabbed my hand and led me to the dance floor. A lot of the kids who had been dancing were leaving now, and a whole bunch of other couples were fighting their way past them and onto the floor. Denyse walked into the very middle. That was good. We'd have a protective layer of other dancers around us so we wouldn't be obvious for everybody to stare at.

Denyse stopped, spun around, and looped her arms around my neck. I put my arms around her, careful of where I was touching and how close I was to places I shouldn't be touching. I felt sweat start to drip from my armpits and tried desperately to remember if I'd put on deodorant that morning.

"Bridget and I are going to the movies tonight," Denyse said. "She said that you and Steve might be going as well."

"I don't know about Steve, but I'm not going."

"You're not?" She sounded disappointed.

"I was going to, but my father's flying in tonight and my mom and I are going to meet him at the airport. He's been away on business for nearly two weeks," I explained, so I wouldn't sound too sucky for going to the airport.

"I'm sure he'll be happy to see you."

"Besides, I have to get to bed early tonight because we're going up to the resort tomorrow."

"Resort?"

"It's a ski club. My family are members."

"I didn't think there was much skiing around here," Denyse said.

"There isn't. That's why we have to get up early to go north ... it's about a three-hour drive."

"Have you been skiing long?" she asked.

"Since I was little, but I don't really ski much any more. I board."

"Boarding is cool."

"You board?" I asked.

"No, but it *looks* cool."

"It is!" I exclaimed. "A whole lot of the tricks you do are exactly the same as in rollerblading."

"So who brings along the first-aid kit for you?" Denyse asked.

"First-aid kit? Why would we need a ... ? Oh, yeah, right." I guess she wasn't about to forget my face plant on the road in front of her house.

"I've always wanted to try boarding," Denyse said.

"Would you like to come with me tomorrow?" The words had jumped out of my mouth so fast that it was like I'd heard them before I'd even thought them.

"I'd like to," Denyse said, "but I have basketball practice tomorrow."

"Oh, that's too bad." I felt the double emotion of disappointment and relief, combined with a tinge of embarrassment. I'd invited her and she'd turned me down.

"But you know, I haven't missed a practice all year long," Denyse said. "Maybe, just this once, I could skip it. What time would I have to be ready?"

"We're going to leave around six."

"In the morning?"

"It's a long drive, so we have to leave early to get time on the slopes."

She nodded her head. "Then I'll be ready."

Denyse put her head against my shoulder and her hair brushed against my cheek. It did feel different. Different, but good. Really good.

# CHAPTER NINE

"WHEN I SAID you could bring a friend, I didn't realize that we'd be filling the van up," my father said as we pulled out of the driveway early the next morning.

"I didn't think it would matter," I said.

"Besides," Steve said from the back seat, "Tom needs me along to do the smooth talking."

"You're certainly good at that, Steve," my father agreed.

"But it is okay for me to invite three people … right?"

"Of course. I was just giving you a hard time."

I'd invited Denyse, and then Steve, and then I'd figured I should invite Bridget, to keep Steve happy.

"Remember, boys, I'm old, but I wasn't born old. I know that it's always nice to have a friend along when you go out, sort of like a double date."

"It isn't a date," I replied.

"Speak for yourself," Steve said. "Bridget and I are on a date."

"Does she know that?" I asked.

"Not yet, but she will."

"Turn here," I said to my father. "This is Denyse's street."

"That's convenient," my father chuckled. "You could walk here in no time."

"That's her house, right there ... with the basketball hoop."

My father slowed down and pulled into the driveway. I was just about to get out to ring the doorbell when Bridget appeared. Denyse had invited her to sleep over because of the early start. She was carrying a snowboard with her.

My father leaned closer to me. "I can see why you like her. She's *very* pretty."

"That's not Denyse, that's Bridget," Steve said. "And you're seeing why *I* like her."

"There's Denyse," I said as she followed Bridget down the driveway.

"That's Denyse?" my father asked.

"Yeah," Steve said. "She's pretty too."

"Yes ... yes she is," my father said, but with a little hesitation. I was pretty sure I knew what had thrown him, but I wasn't going to mention it.

"Can you flip open the back door?" I asked.

My father reached over and hit the button that released the back doors of the van. Steve and I climbed out.

"Good morning!" I called.

"It's certainly an early morning," Denyse replied.

"Here, let me take your board," Steve offered as he grabbed Bridget's board and put it in the back of the van. "Do you board a lot?"

"I've only been a couple of times this year, but last winter I went practically every weekend," she replied.

"That's great, so you're already an expert."

"I'm pretty good."

"You didn't tell me that," Denyse said. "I thought you were a beginner too."

"Didn't you wonder when she brought over her own board?" Steve asked.

"I just thought she'd borrowed one. So, you three all know what you're doing."

"Don't worry, Denyse," Steve said. "It's really easy, and Tom is a great teacher, so I'm sure you'll be boarding like a pro by noon."

I nodded my head. "I'll show you how to do it. You'll be up and making runs before you know it."

"If you all don't get into the van right away we won't be making any runs at all today," my father called out.

We all climbed in, me up front and Steve and the girls in the back. That was probably the only time in my life that I was sorry I was sitting in the front seat. We started off.

"So, is anybody going to do the introductions?"

"Sorry. Dad, this is Denyse and Bridget. Denyse and Bridget, this is my dad, Mr. Martin."

"Good to meet you, sir," Denyse said. "And thank you so much for allowing us to come with you this morning."

"You're very welcome, Denyse. My wife told me how polite you are."

Mom had told him a lot of things, I guess, but apparently hadn't mentioned that she was black.

Then again, neither had I. Maybe I should have. Maybe it shouldn't have mattered. Maybe it didn't matter.

"YOU'RE DOING REALLY WELL," I said, encouragingly.

"If this is good, I'd hate to see bad," Denyse replied. "I must have fallen down a hundred times."

"Not that many times, and you didn't fall at all the last two runs down the bunny hill."

"I guess you're right."

"It's a combination of a good student and a good teacher. Now I think you're ready to try something a little more challenging."

"I am?"

"Sure. We should head to the bigger hills."

"Bigger? How much bigger?"

"Not too big. Besides, the bigger hills are actually easier than the small ones."

"*Sure* ...," she said, sarcastically.

"I'm not kidding! Going down the small hills is like riding a bike really, really slowly. You start to wobble and then fall down. The speed helps keep you on your feet."

"That's a great theory … you're sure?"

"Trust me. And remember, if you're going too fast then just—"

"Fall down."

"Exactly!"

She shook her head. "Strangest sport in the world, where falling down is the best way to save yourself."

"No more tow rope," I said. "Bigger hills mean the chairlift. Come on."

I glided away on my board, pushing with my free foot. Denyse came behind me slowly. We got into the lineup for the lift and shuffled forward until we were first.

"Wait until the chair passes and then scoot up to that line," I directed her.

Denyse nodded and gave me a weak little smile. She looked nervous.

"Ready … now!" I said as the chair passed. I glided and I could see she was struggling so I reached over, grabbed her by the arm, and pulled her into position.

"Now lean back … and here it comes!"

The chair bumped against the backs of our legs and Denyse let out a little yelp as we sat down. It rocked us a bit as we rose into the air.

"I'm going to bring down the safety bar now," I said. I reached up and lowered it into position.

"Thanks," Denyse said. "I really don't like heights that much."

"I'm not crazy about them either, but this chair doesn't get too high. I think forty or fifty feet, tops."

"That sounds pretty high to me and—what was that?" The chair had just clattered over the tower.

"That was nothing, don't worry."

"I *am* worried, and it wasn't nothing."

"It's the sound the chair will make every time we go over a tower. That should be the least of your worries."

"So what *should* I be worried about?" Denyse asked. I suppose I wasn't making her feel any better.

"Sorry, that was just a figure of speech."

"You're sure nothing is going to—?" Denyse stopped mid-sentence as the chair came to an abrupt halt and we rocked forward. "Oh my God!" She grabbed my hand, and I could feel her digging in her fingernails right through the glove.

"It's nothing!" I exclaimed. "They just stopped the chair—somebody must have fallen."

"Somebody fell from the lift?" Denyse pushed herself back into the seat.

"Not from up here. When they were getting on or off. Getting off is when people tend to fall the most."

"Oh, great, something to look forward to."

"You won't fall," I said. "I won't let you fall. You just hang onto me and I'll keep you up."

"Promise?"

"I promise."

This was a big promise to make, since I'd often seen one person trying to hold up another until they both fell down together into a tangled pile of arms and legs.

The chair started to move again. I was very aware that, while she'd loosened her death-grip, Denyse was still holding my hand. I figured she was still pretty scared.

"Have you noticed the mix of people here today?" she asked.

"I guess they're the usual people." In honesty, I'd been concentrating so much on Denyse I hadn't noticed anybody else at all.

"So there usually aren't any black people at this place?" Denyse asked.

So that's what she meant. "I'm not sure."

"Look around," she said. "My face is the only one here that's not the same colour as the snow."

"I never noticed."

"You would if you were black."

I gave her a questioning look.

"You wouldn't understand," she said, looking away.

"I might if you tried to explain it to me," I snapped.

She didn't answer right away, but I could tell by the look on her face when she turned back that she was thinking about what to say.

"You have to understand that the world is basically white," Denyse began.

"I thought it was mainly covered by water and was blue," I joked.

"Do you want to make bad jokes or do you want an answer?"

"Sorry."

"Most of the places I go—*all* the places I go— there are always a lot more white people than black. Think about our neighbourhood, our school."

"Yeah, I guess so. But does that matter?"

"Of course it matters. At least it matters to some people," Denyse answered.

"It doesn't matter to me," I replied. "Black or white. It's not like I go around counting them."

"I do."

"You do?"

"Not always, but a lot of the time," she said. "And you do too, sometimes."

"No I don't," I argued.

"Yeah? How many players on your rep team are white and how many are black?"

"Well ..."

"Are you telling me that you don't know, or that you haven't noticed?" she demanded.

Of course she was right. I did know. There were seven black players and five white guys.

"I've got to raise the bar now," I said, instead of answering her.

"What?" Denyse asked.

"The bar. I have to raise it so we can get off the chair." I lifted it up. "Now, edge toward the front of the seat and let the chair sort of push

you on the bottom and I'll pull you by the hand.
Ready? … Now!"

We jumped off the chair and started down the
little slope as the chair spun around behind us and
started back down the hill. Denyse waved her
free hand in the air as she tried to keep her
balance. I kept my grip on her and held her up,
and together we glided away from the chair,
staying up and on our boards.

"Congratulations! That's the hardest part of
boarding, and you did it!"

"Thanks, but can we sit down for a minute?"

"Sure." We went over to a bench at the top of
the hill, off to one side.

"I just need to catch my breath," she said.

"That's okay. You need to sit down anyway, to
strap in your free foot. Now remember, we're
not going for speed records on this hill. We're
just going to make lots of slow, gentle passes,
going across the hill as much as we go down it.
Understand?"

She nodded.

"And if it starts to feel like you're going too
fast or you're getting scared or out of control,
then just fall down."

"That's the one part I've really mastered," she joked.

I smiled, and she smiled back. The tension that had been between us had vanished.

"Let's go. Follow my line down the hill."

We got up and started down the slope. I followed a gentle line, making sure we would have enough speed to board but not enough to feel out of control. I looked over my shoulder. Denyse was on her feet and not far behind. I reached the side of the slope and cut back across the face. Denyse did the same.

"Way to go!" I yelled over my shoulder.

We kept cutting back and forth across the hill as boarders and skiers shot past us. The good news was that we were moving so slowly it was easy for them to avoid us. Finally we glided to the bottom of the hill and onto the flat at the end. I did a little jump stop.

"Congratulations on staying up for your first—"

"Look out!" Denyse screamed as she bowled into me, and we crashed together into a jumble of arms and legs.

"I'm so sorry!" she said as she tried to untangle herself.

"That's okay," I told her, rolling over in the snow to get out from under her as quickly as possible. "I did tell you to fall if you needed to. I guess I should have mentioned not to fall on *me*."

"Or maybe you should have taught me how to stop better! Are you all right?"

"I'm fine. You've seen me take a worse fall than that," I joked.

Denyse tried to get up but we were still so tangled that it wasn't working.

"Hold still," I ordered, "and I'll get us free."

I reached down and released one of my feet from the bindings. Then I undid the other. I got to my knees, and as I bent forward I found myself almost nose to nose with Denyse. I looked down, she looked up, and she smelled so good that I leaned forward and … we kissed!

# *CHAPTER TEN*

I PULLED AWAY from the kiss. "I'm so sorry!" I blurted out.

"You're *sorry*?" Denyse questioned.

I nodded my head. "I shouldn't have done that!"

"Why not?" she asked. "Am I a bad kisser?"

"No, of course not! I mean I shouldn't have just kissed you like that. I should have asked or something."

Denyse smiled. "It was okay for you to kiss me." She reached up and put a hand on the back of my neck and pulled me closer, and we kissed again! This time we held the kiss longer, and I was more aware of her lips against my lips and her hand on the back of my neck. She released me and we separated.

"Are you still sorry?" she asked.

"Of course not!"

"Good, because neither am I. But we'd better get untangled and off the hill before somebody smashes into us."

"Yeah, sure." In the excitement of the kiss I'd forgotten where we were. Skiers and boarders were buzzing around us on all sides.

I reached down and released Denyse's feet from the bindings. We stood up and grabbed our boards.

"Do you want to take a break?" I suggested.

"I could use a drink."

We walked over to the chalet and left our boards against the racks. I opened up the door and a rush of warm air greeted us. The chalet was warm and crowded and noisy.

"How about if I get us something to drink and you go and try to find seats," I said.

Denyse reached over and gave my hand a little squeeze and a surge of electricity shot up my arm. I stood there watching as she walked away. She looked back at me over her shoulder and flashed a beautiful smile before she turned a corner and was gone.

Wow. I'd kissed Denyse. And even better, Denyse had kissed me. What did I do next? I wished Steve were with me now. He'd had a lot more experience in this sort of thing than I had. He could tell me what to do, or what not to do, because not only had he had a lot of girlfriends but he'd made just about every mistake possible in dealing with them. You can learn a lot by making mistakes ... or even by watching other people make mistakes.

I cut around the big line waiting for food and went to the drink dispensers. I grabbed two medium cups and then put them back and grabbed two large cups instead. I didn't want her to think I was cheap. I put some ice in the bottom of both cups and then filled them to the top with Coke. Funny how I already knew what she liked without having to ask her. I'd heard that couples were like that. Couples ... were we a couple?

I paid for the drinks and went out into the seating area. I saw Denyse at the end of a large table.

"These are practically the only two free seats in the whole place," she said.

"That's because a lot of people spend more time sitting around than they do skiing or boarding."

"And I guess other people never come in," Denyse said. "Some of those guys out there must be skiing or boarding all the time to get that good."

"Yeah, some people are up here every weekend, all winter long," I said.

"Would you like to do that?"

"I like boarding, but I like other things, too. Besides, there's all the other stuff in life that you have to do, whether you like it or not."

"Like homework," Denyse said.

"Homework I can handle. Tomorrow I have to go to church."

"I didn't know you belonged to a church."

"First Methodist, just over from the school," I answered.

"Do you go very often?"

"Thank goodness only about once a month."

"That's not bad. I have to go every Sunday," Denyse said.

"Every Sunday! That seems extreme."

"I agree, but I'm in the choir. Tomorrow I have a bit of a solo."

"You sing?" I asked.

"I try."

"I bet you're good. What church do you belong to?"

"The Baptist Church of the Nazarene."

"I don't know that one."

"It's not even in town. It's out in the city."

"That's a long way to go to church. Why do you travel there?" I asked.

"No choice. My father is the pastor."

"Your father is a minister?"

"Yeah. Surprised?"

"I guess. I don't know anybody else whose father is a pastor or a minister or a rabbi or anything like that."

"Me neither," Denyse agreed.

"It must be ... different."

She shrugged. "I don't know, because it's all I've ever known. Would you like to hear me sing?"

"Here?" I asked, looking around the crowded room.

"Of course not. I mean at church. Would you like to come to church with me tomorrow? That is, if your parents would let you."

"They'd let me."

"So, do you want to come?"

"I'd like that," I told her. What was I saying?

"Great. My dad leaves really early, way before seven, but you can ride in with me and my mom and brother."

"Jamar?"

"Yeah."

"He doesn't strike me as the church-going type."

"He has no choice. In my family, you *have* to be the church-going type. At least it isn't so bad these days. When my oldest brothers were little the whole family had to sit through three services every Sunday. And then on special occasions, like Easter or Christmas, there would be extra ones."

My eyes widened in surprise and horror.

"And if you think it's boring to have to sit through one church service, think about what it would be like to hear the same sermon *three or four times*."

"That would be like torture."

"And to make it even worse, we almost always know what the sermon is going to be about because Dad writes and practises it all week long."

"That would be tough." I paused. "Are you sure it's okay with your parents for me to go along?"

"Why are you asking—have I scared you off?" Denyse asked.

"No. I want to go. At least, I want to go to your church more than I want to go to mine. I was just wondering if it would be okay."

"It'll be fine. I bring friends all the time."

"Okay, then it's a date." I felt myself start to blush. "You know what I mean."

"I know. So, ready to get back out on the slopes?"

"Definitely."

"Listen, I think I've had enough thrills and excitement for a while. Would you mind if I went back to the bunny hill?" Denyse asked.

"No, if that's what you want."

"You look a little disappointed," she said.

"Not really … I guess."

"I suppose the bunny hill isn't where you normally spend your time."

"Not since I was four years old. I'm usually at the terrain park."

"The terrain park?" she asked.

"It's for boarders and ski-bladers who want to do tricks. It has a half-pipe and jumps and some rails for grinding."

"Is that where Steve and Bridget are now?"

"I'm not sure, but probably."

"And that's where you'd be if I weren't here, right?"

"Definitely," I said, and instantly realized I'd said it too enthusiastically. "But that doesn't mean that I'm not happy to be here, because I am. Really."

"Really?"

"Yeah."

"Still, it doesn't seem fair. How about if we finish our drinks and I go back to the bunny hill and you go to the terrain park for a while."

"No, I'll stay with you."

"I really think you should go. I'll be fine. Maybe better than fine—I won't be so nervous about falling down without you there watching. So go … please."

"Are you sure?"

"Positive," she said, flashing me a smile.

"I won't be gone long. I'll just do a few runs and be right back."

"Take your time. Have some fun. It's not like I can't use the practice."

"Okay. I'll be back in an hour. If that's okay?"

"It's more than okay."

I hesitated.

Denyse reached up, threw her arms around my neck, and gave me a kiss. "Now go."

I WAITED FOR THE BOARDER ahead of me to get far enough along before I dropped into the half-pipe. He climbed up the side of the pipe, grabbed some air, and then shot over the rim, landing in a heap on the top. Looked good for me to go now. As I started down I began to think about all the advice I'd given to Denyse, explaining things to her. My head felt all cluttered with thoughts, and that wasn't good. Boarding was about doing, not thinking. I pushed the thoughts out of my mind as I scaled one wall, caught a little air, and then came down, hitting the other side and doing a 180 spin. I picked up speed as I left the end of the pipe and headed for one of the jumps. I hit it and did a two-handed grab! Too bad Denyse wasn't around to see that!

"Tom!"

I turned and caught sight of Steve sitting on his board at the side of the slope. I pulled up and off to the side to meet him. He was by himself.

"Bridget get tired of you already?" I asked.

"She went to the washroom—again. I think that girl must have a bladder problem."

"I kissed her," I blurted out.

"Bridget?"

"No, of course not. Denyse!" I said.

"Where?" Steve demanded.

"Here ... right on the slopes."

"I didn't mean that. I meant, like, where did you kiss her, you know, the cheek, the lips— where?"

"The lips," I said proudly.

"And did she kiss you back?" Steve asked.

"Twice."

Steve reached over and gave me a slap on the back. "I wouldn't have bet any money on you getting kissed before me today. Way to go, Tom." He paused. "So, did you slip her the tongue?"

"Steve! Give me a break! Don't you think that's a little personal?"

"That's why I asked. Besides, she's probably in the washroom with Bridget right now telling her the whole story."

"She's not even in the washroom. I left her on the slopes."

"This slope?" Steve asked.

"No, the bunny hill."

"You left her on the bunny hill and you came here?" he asked in disbelief.

"Yeah … "

"And you don't see a problem with that?" Steve questioned.

"No."

"You left her alone, by herself, while you wandered away, and you don't think that is a problem?"

"It was her idea that I go. She suggested it."

Steve shook his head slowly. "For a smart guy, you certainly aren't very bright. She only suggested that so you could turn her down."

"Why would she do that?" I asked.

"Because she's supposed to ask, so that you turn her down, so then she knows how much you like being with her."

"That sounds crazy."

"Of course it sounds crazy, but it's true."

"Are you sure?" I asked.

"Am I ever wrong when it comes to girls?" Steve asked.

"Most of the time."

"Well, not this time. Believe me. I did this one wrong myself twice before I figured it out. Remember Allison?"

"Vaguely."

"That's because she dumped me. How long have you been gone?"

"About fifteen minutes."

"And how long does she expect you to be gone?" Steve asked.

"Around an hour."

"Then there's still hope. Go back, right now, and tell her you'd rather be doing something you *don't* like with her than doing something you like *without* her."

"You don't actually expect me to say that, do you?" I asked.

"Depends on whether you want those first kisses to be your last kisses as well. Apologize— a lot—and get going!"

I CAME TO A STOP at the bottom of the bunny hill. I scanned the slope. If Denyse was up there I certainly couldn't see her. Maybe she was on the tow rope on her way up, or maybe she'd gone back to the chalet. I turned toward the chalet and that's when I saw her, sitting on a bench. I waved to her, but she didn't respond. Either she hadn't seen me or Steve was right and she was too annoyed at me to wave back.

I slid toward her and tried desperately to remember what Steve had told me to tell her. All I could remember was that I thought what he'd suggested was stupid. Of course, stupid might be better than nothing, which was what I had now. I stopped right in front of her. She looked angry, and that angry look didn't change to acknowledge that I was even there. I cleared my throat and she looked up.

"I must have lost track of time," she said. "Has it been an hour already?"

"Not even close. I came back early. Way early." What was it that Steve had told me to say … oh, yeah. "I'd rather be here with you not enjoying myself than enjoying myself at the terrain park."

"You aren't enjoying being with me?" She looked like she was about to cry.

"No, no, of course not!" I exclaimed. "I *like* being with you! I'd rather be here with you on the bunny slope than at the terrain park by myself because I like being with you!" That sounded better!

"That's so sweet," she said, and her face broke into a smile—a smile I was very grateful to see.

It was looking as though Steve actually knew what he was talking about this time. Now I had to apologize.

"I'm really sorry about leaving you."

"That's all right."

"I didn't mean to make you angry."

"You didn't," she said.

"Or ... sad."

"No, you were right the first time, I'm angry, but not at you."

"You sure?"

She nodded her head.

I was so relieved that it wasn't me that I almost didn't want to ask her who she *was* angry at, but I knew I had to.

"Who ticked you off?"

"Some jerk. Some old jerk man."

"I had the jerk part figured out already. What did he do?"

"It's not what he did, it's what he said."

"What did he say?" I asked. Sometimes the members of the club could be pretty snotty with guests, especially guests who were teenagers.

"Forget it," she said, and her expression hardened again.

I was actually just as happy to forget it. Unless this was like me going off by myself and I was *supposed* to ask her again.

"What did he say?" I asked. "Please tell me."

She took a deep breath. "He said ... he said," her voice barely above a whisper, "that he knew the club had a bunny hill ... but he didn't know that it had a jungle bunny on it."

I gasped. "Somebody really said that?"

"You think I'm making it up?" Denyse demanded.

"Of course not! It's just hard to believe that anybody would say something like that! I know a lot of these people ... I know most of them. And I've never heard anybody say anything like that before!"

"I've heard that kind of thing before, and a lot worse."

"Show me the guy," I said. "Show me who said that to you."

Denyse shook her head.

"Why not?"

"Because then you'd feel like you had to go over and punch him or something."

"I wouldn't punch him, but I would go and tell him off," I said.

"It could just end up with somebody punching somebody, and it wouldn't make it any better. You have to learn to ignore the idiots of the world."

"I don't know if I can do that," I said.

"You'll have to learn to ignore them if you want to be my boyfriend."

"Your boyfriend?"

"You do want to be my boyfriend, don't you?"

"Yeah ... that would be nice," I answered.

"Good. Because I don't just go around kissing boys."

"Me neither—I mean *girls*! I don't just go around kissing girls!" I sputtered.

Denyse laughed. That was a big relief!

"I bet you've kissed more girls than I've kissed boys," she said.

"Don't bet what you can't afford to lose," I said. Denyse was only the third girl I'd ever kissed, if you didn't count cousins, aunts, my sister, and my mother.

"It's a bet I can't lose," Denyse said.

"Don't be so sure."

"I am. The worst I can do is a tie," Denyse said.

"What does that mean?" I asked.

Denyse's eyes were on the ground, and then she shyly looked up at me. "That was my first kiss."

"Wow."

She smiled. "Did I do okay?"

"Better than okay," I said. "But you know it's probably like everything else. The more you practise, the better you get. I have an idea." I paused. "Maybe we should kiss until you make six in a row."

# *CHAPTER ELEVEN*

"STAND STILL so I can get this on right," my father said as he tried to straighten the tie around my neck.

"I don't even see why I have to wear it," I protested.

"Two reasons. One, because you're going to church, and two, because your mother said you have to wear a tie." He fiddled with the tie. He was having trouble making the two ends even.

"So, I guess you really like this Denyse girl," he said.

"I do."

"You must. The first girl I ever went to church with was your mother. And that was the day we got married."

"Well, we're not getting married."

"That's good to hear, because last time I checked you were still thirteen, and isn't she younger than you?"

"One year."

"It's hard to tie a tie on somebody else," my father said. He pulled the tie off me and wrapped it around his own neck. "Did she enjoy being at the resort yesterday?"

"I think so. At least most of it."

"Really? What's not to like?"

"Somebody said something to her. Something racist."

My father stopped fussing with the tie for a second. He nodded his head. "That's sad, but not altogether surprising."

"It isn't?"

"Our club, a long time ago, a long, *long* time before we were ever members, was restricted."

"Restricted to what?"

"Restricted to whites."

"Come on, you're joking, right?"

"No, I'm not. There were lots of places like that. Ski resorts, golf courses, private clubs, you name it."

"But that's, like, ancient history," I argued.

"Not that ancient. There are some people in our club who were members when it was restricted, who probably still think it *should* be."

"That's stupid!" I snapped.

"Hey, don't get mad at me. It wasn't my idea. And it isn't restricted now," my father said.

"So anybody can join, right?"

"Anybody who has the money and is sponsored by an existing member."

"Are there any black families who are members now?" I asked, although I was pretty sure I knew the answer.

"I don't think so," my father answered, "but they'd be free to join if they wanted to."

"So we could sponsor Denyse's family?"

"We could, if they have the money and the interest. But I bet they're not that interested in skiing."

"How can you be so sure they'd don't ski?" I asked, a tinge of anger in my voice. I didn't like the way this was going.

"Well, I know that Denyse doesn't ski, and you just taught her how to board, so I assume nobody in her family does, either." My father paused. "You're sounding angry again."

"I'm not angry," I replied. "I was just thinking that you thought ... no, forget it."

"That I thought that they wouldn't ski just because they're black?" he asked.

Reluctantly I nodded my head. I felt a bit ashamed for even thinking that about my father.

He pulled the tie off over his head and handed it back to me. I brought it over my head and he tugged and snugged it into place.

"There, that looks okay." He paused. I had a feeling we weren't through with this conversation. "Look, Tom, I know that black people can ski and swim. Remember when that sportscaster got fired for saying that black people have heavier bones and that's why they can't swim? I hope you don't think I'm that stupid! But I also know that there do appear to be more black athletes in some sports than others. You know, there are a lot of black track, football, and especially basketball stars, and not so many in tennis, golf, hockey, or Olympic swimming events."

"Well, maybe there would be more if more black members got sponsored into clubs like ours," I suggested.

"There probably would be, and if you know any black families that want into our club, I'll happily sponsor them."

"You'd do that?" I asked.

"You know me well enough to know the answer to that."

He was right. He'd always treated everybody fairly. I'd never heard him, or my mother, ever say anything that was racist about anybody. I couldn't even imagine him doing that.

"I'm glad you're okay about me having Denyse as my girlfriend."

My father looked up. "When did that happen?"

"You mean the girlfriend part?"

He nodded.

"Yesterday. You're okay with that … right?"

He didn't answer right away, like he was think-ing about his answer. That bothered me.

"I'm not *not* okay with it," he finally said.

"What does that mean?"

"It's hard to explain."

"Try."

He let out a big sigh. "Denyse seems like a very nice girl."

"She is."

"I'm glad. I just assumed she had to be nice or she wouldn't be your friend." He paused. "And she's always welcome in this house and at our club."

"And ... ?" I asked, because it sounded as though he'd stopped in the middle of a thought.

"And you're free to date whoever you want. But you have to know that it can be a lot more complicated if one of you is white and the other is black."

"I don't know why it should be," I argued.

"It is. Believe me, it just is. And because you're my son and I love you, I'd rather have things go as simply and easily as possible for you. There are enough complications in life without looking for new ones."

"So what are we talking about here—about people making stupid remarks, like that guy at the resort? Or do you think we're going to be thrown out of restaurants or something? This isn't the sixties, you know. All that's over. Nobody cares any more."

"Sometimes people don't change so much as hide their feelings. And what about Denyse's family?"

"Dad, her father's a minister. I don't think there's a problem in her house.'

"You're probably right. I just don't want to see you get hurt."

"Are you saying I *shouldn't* date Denyse?"

"I didn't say that. I'm only saying it would be easier if Denyse were white."

"So it *does* matter to you!" I exclaimed.

"I'm not saying it's wrong or worse, just more complicated. Nothing more. Nothing less. You date who you want. But go into it with your eyes wide open. That's all. Understand?"

"I guess."

"And you're okay with what I've said?" my father asked.

"I don't know if 'okay' is the right word, but I get what you're saying and I know you're saying it because you care."

"Fair enough," he said.

I heard the doorbell ring.

"That's probably your ride. Be good, be polite, and here's something for the collection plate." He pressed a twenty-dollar bill into my hand.

"Thanks."

"And I'm now going to do you an even bigger favour," my father said. "I'm not going to go down to the door and embarrass you by meeting Denyse's mother and saying all sorts of stupid things."

"Dad, you have no idea how much I appreciate that."

"Right. I'm going to leave that job to your mother." He grinned. "Now, go downstairs before she has a chance to start telling that story about how you wouldn't go to kindergarten without your teddy bear!"

I took my father's advice and hurried to the door. My mother, Denyse, and another woman who had to be Denyse's mother stood at the door. Both Denyse and her mother were all dressed up. Maybe wearing a tie wasn't such a bad idea.

"And this, of course, is my Thomas," my mother said.

"Hi. Pleased to meet you, Mrs. Smith," I said, extending my hand to shake.

"I'm pleased to meet you too, young man."

"I was just telling Sharon that this is the only time in your entire life that you've ever asked to go to church," my mother said. She turned to Denyse's mother. "He tends to drift off during the service, so if he starts to snore just reach over and give him a little kick in the shins."

"I won't fall asleep!" I protested. "I'm sure I'll really like the sermon."

My mother laughed. "That would be a first! Then again, I haven't heard too many thrilling sermons myself."

"But this one will be good, right, Denyse?" I asked, looking for support.

She shook her head. "I've heard bits of it all week and it's not what I'd call one of my father's best."

My mother looked confused.

"Denyse's father is the pastor of their church," I explained.

"Oh, my goodness ... I didn't mean to imply that your husband's sermons aren't good," my mother sputtered.

Denyse's mother put a hand on my mother's shoulder. "I've been married to him for twenty-three years and I've heard every sermon he's ever given, and *believe me*, honey, there have only been a few that even the most devoted wife would call 'thrilling.'"

They both laughed, and the tension in the air vanished.

"Now, we'd better get going. We sit right up front, and people tend to notice if we come in partway through the service."

"It was nice to meet you," my mother said as the two women shook hands again.

My mother came over and gave me a kiss on the cheek and a hug. "Be good ... stay awake," she whispered in my ear.

I followed Denyse out to the car. Jamar was sitting in the front passenger seat. He was dressed in a suit and he looked to be asleep, all slumped over with a baseball cap pulled down over his face. Denyse and I climbed into the back seat. I closed the door as quietly as possible——keeping Jamar asleep seemed like a good idea to me. We put on our seatbelts and Denyse reached over and gave my hand a squeeze. Yesterday when she did that I liked it, but now, with her family in the car, it made me feel just a little ... uncomfortable.

"So, Thomas, what church does your family attend?"

"The Methodist church here in town."

"That means your minister is Reverend Hurley."

"Yes, he is." I wondered how she knew that.

"He and his wife have been to our house for dinner. We tend to get to know all the other clergy in town. They're nice people ... but of course you knew that already."

"Yeah," I replied, although I'd never said anything more than "Good morning" to our minister on the way out of church.

"I should warn you," Denyse's mother said, "that our church services are a little different from the ones you're used to."

Almost anything would have been better, so I figured different wasn't a bad thing. Denyse reached out again and took my hand. This time she didn't let go.

WE JOINED A LINE of cars waiting to turn into the parking lot of the church. There was also a line waiting to get out—people who'd been at the earlier service. We found a parking spot by the front door of the church. Denyse opened the door and she and I climbed out of the car.

"Time to get up," Denyse's mother said as she gave Jamar a little shake.

"How about if I wait out here?" he said, without moving a muscle.

"How about if you come with your father next week and you can sit through all three services?" Mrs. Smith asked.

"I think I'll come right now," he said, as he immediately came to life and jumped out of the car. Denyse's mother hurried into the church as Jamar stretched. He suddenly realized that I was standing there and his expression changed to surprise.

"Where did you come from?"

"He drove in our car," Denyse said. "He's here with us."

Jamar scowled. "He may have come in our car, but he ain't here with me. Meet you at the car after the service."

Jamar walked off and met a bunch of kids about his age who were waiting to go inside. They shook hands and greeted each other like long-lost friends.

"Your brother doesn't seem to like me," I said.

"Don't take it personally. He's just way, way too cool to be seen with me, either. He has his rep to protect, and being seen with little sisters or younger guys doesn't fit the image he's trying to build."

As we walked up the steps, I immediately noticed one of the ways that this church was different from mine. Every single person—young, old, babies, male, female, going into church or coming out of church—was black. Was I the only white person there? Maybe there were some already inside.

It also became apparent as we walked inside that Denyse knew most of the people we passed. They greeted her, touched her arm, and some even gave her a hug. She introduced me to people and everybody seemed very friendly, very warm.

"You'll be sitting with my mother," Denyse said.

"Don't you mean *we'll* be sitting with your mother?"

"No," she said, shaking her head. "You'll be sitting with my mother and I'll be sitting up there," she said, pointing to the choir loft. "I'm singing, remember?"

"I remember. I just hadn't thought it through. Where will your brother be sitting?"

"Somewhere toward the back. Maybe in the parking lot, if nobody notices. Why, do you want to sit with him?" She grinned.

"No, just wondering."

Denyse led me to the very first pew. Her mother was already seated. "See you after the service," she said.

As I sat down an organ began to play. Denyse's mother leaned in close. "I'll give you an elbow if you fall asleep, if you do the same for me. It looks very poor if the pastor's wife takes a nap during his sermon."

From the back of the church the choir began to sing. I turned and watched as, two by two, the members of the choir began walking up the centre aisle. With each pair the sound grew, getting louder and stronger. Row by row, as the choir passed them, the members of the congregation rose. It was almost as if the strength of the voices was forcing people to their feet. Denyse appeared in the line. I found myself trying hard not to stare at her, but failing miserably. Her eyes caught mine and she smiled as she walked past me and then climbed the stairs to the choir loft.

As the organ stopped playing a man bounded up toward the altar. I recognized him from around the neighbourhood. He was really big, as tall as Jamar and heavier, and his head was shaved … and, of course, he was black. When I'd seen him around town I'd always assumed he was a football player or something like that. Minister had never crossed my mind. So this was Denyse's father. I wouldn't want to get him mad at me.

"Good morning, brothers and sisters!" he called out, and it seemed like the entire congregation yelled back a greeting.

"We are most blessed to find ourselves here today, together in God's house and in God's love!"

"Hallelujah!" called out a voice from the congregation.

"Let us start this day by making a joyous noise!" the pastor called out, and suddenly the whole church was filled with the sound of music. I spun around. Off to one side was a band—no, an orchestra! There were drums, a guitar, a bass, a couple of trumpets, a trombone, and a sax! They were playing a song that was like nothing I'd ever heard in church before! The music kept building and building and building, and just when I thought it couldn't get any stronger the choir jumped in and practically took the roof off the place! From behind me came the voices of the congregation joining in. Some of the people had risen to their feet, and others were in the aisles, swaying and moving to the sound!

I looked all around at the people. Almost without exception everybody was really well dressed—dressed fancy. A lot of the women wore hats and gloves. There were a lot more women than men, but I guess that wasn't so different from my church.

In the last row I saw a white face, a woman. In her arms was a baby. He couldn't have been more than six or eight months old. He was sort of black and sort of white-looking. I had this strange urge to wave to her. Was that what Denyse had meant about counting the black faces?

The song came to an end and there was a roar of cheers and applause. The pastor came back to the lectern. He took a sip from a glass of water. "I read the newspapers yesterday," he began. "They call it news, but nothing in there seemed to be new." He paused. "The same things keep happening. Again and again and again. The night before last, a young man was killed by a police officer. The young man was black. The police officer was white."

I felt a shiver go up my spine as people yelled things out—"Isn't it always that way?" "Where's the justice?" Suddenly I felt much whiter and much more alone.

"The young man who was killed was twenty-one years old, the age of my oldest son. He could have been my son, but he wasn't." The pastor paused. "But he was my brother."

"And mine too!" yelled a voice.

"And what of the policeman—the white policeman—who fired the fatal shot? What is to become of him?"

"Nothing!" screamed an angry voice.

The pastor shook his head sadly. "They say they're going to be giving him a medal," he said in a hushed voice. There were gasps from behind me. "And do you know why they're going to give him a medal?" he asked, his voice suddenly as loud as thunder. "Do you know why?"

More screamed replies from the congregation, so many that I couldn't make out any individual's words. I slumped lower in the pew, wondering if the woman at the back had been able to slip out, but not wanting to risk looking back to find out.

"The reason they're going to give him a medal is simple. He's getting that medal because he *deserves* to receive that medal. He earned that medal, and I would be honoured to be there to shake that young man's hand!"

There was stunned silence, as if nobody could believe what he'd just said, as if all the air had been sucked out of people's lungs and they couldn't even gasp again.

"The young man—the young black man who was killed—was all hyped up on drugs. They think it was crack. He'd already taken the life of his own four-year-old son, and he was holding a knife to the throat of that child's mother. He was saying he was going to kill her. The policeman— little more than a boy himself at only twenty-three years of age—had spent almost two hours trying to talk the man into giving up the knife, into allowing that young black woman to live. At risk of his own life, he tried to save the lives of both the woman and the man who held her hostage. When he couldn't, when the knife slashed that woman's throat, he had no choice and he fired his gun. But he fired it not to take a life, he fired it to save a life. The life of that young

woman. And after firing that fatal shot he then
pressed his hands against the throat of that
woman, trying to stop her lifeblood from flowing
out of her body, through his fingers, and onto the
ground. And he stayed with her—there, in the
ambulance, and right into the operating room.
They say—the doctors who operated on her—
that if not for his actions she would certainly have
died. And for that he is a hero. Because that girl
was not my daughter, but she was my sister."

He paused and took another sip from the glass
perched precariously on the edge of the lectern.

"Now, I know what you're thinking. So often it
has been an innocent black man killed by a white
police officer—the man's crime simply to be
black—a victim of racism, a disease that is crip-
pling this country. But if you think ... think long
and hard ... weren't you just as guilty of an act of
racism when you assumed that the policeman in
my story was guilty simply because of the colour
of his skin?

"Now, in truth, your thoughts didn't cause a
death, but thoughts lead to actions, and actions
start to take on a life of their own that could end
a life."

He stopped and took another drink of water. He then removed a white handkerchief from his jacket pocket and slowly, deliberately, began to mop his brow.

"Has anybody here ever wondered what colour God is?"

I'd never really even thought to ask that question because I'd just assumed he was white, like Jesus and Moses and all the other guys from the Bible.

"Look around this world," he continued, "and you can't help but think that God is white ... " He paused. " ... And brown ... and black ... and yellow ... and red. How can He not be all of those colours? Is it not written that we are made in the image of God? That unfortunate, troubled young man who was killed was my brother, and so was his child. The young policeman is also my brother. The woman lying in hospital is my sister. We are all brothers and sisters."

Again he took a sip from his water. I was beginning to realize that he wasn't doing this only because he was thirsty but because it was part of his presentation. This wasn't just a sermon. This was like a performance, a wonderful performance.

I felt myself almost drained, listening, watching, wondering what he was going to say next.

"Now maybe some people—maybe a lot of people—both white and black, don't know or agree with what I have said. In the old days they might have used weapons against us, or thrown rocks, or brought lit torches into our house of worship—and believe me, those days are still a reality in parts of our great country. But now they're more likely to use words as weapons ... to hurl words at you to harm you, to demean, demoralize, or demonize who you are. You must resist the urge to strike back. You must turn the other cheek. I believe most of you have heard of that." He looked up and smiled. "You must have the strength not to lash out against them with the same anger and hatred that they use against you. You must have the strength of Gandhi, or of Dr. King. For you must remember that only love can defeat hate. We were put on this planet to love our neighbours as we love ourselves. When you leave this house of worship today, I implore you to leave in peace and love. Reach out your hand, not to strike in anger but to greet in peace."

He lowered his head and began reciting the Lord's Prayer, and everybody bowed their heads and joined in. I mumbled along, but my mind was resonating with his words. This was the sermon that Denyse didn't think was very good?

"We will now pass the collection plate while the choir sings," the pastor said.

Six people, five women and a man, came to the front and took the collection plates. They split into three pairs and proceeded down the aisles as the band began to play "Amazing Grace" and the choir joined in. It was much quieter than before, but just as beautiful. The collection plate came to me and I dug into my pocket and pulled out the twenty-dollar bill. I dropped it in as a single voice rose above the rest of the choir. I looked up. It was Denyse! She had stepped out in front and was singing a solo. Her voice was soft, but strong and clear. I could hear each word as her voice rose and fell with the notes. And as she sang, there was a look on her face—a look of calm.

The solo ended and as the rest of the choir joined in she stepped back. But as she did she looked directly at me and smiled, and I felt as if my whole body was melting into the pew.

# *CHAPTER TWELVE*

IT WAS A LONG TIME after the service was over before we finally left the church. People kept coming up to Denyse and her mother. Some wanted to talk, others asked questions, and others simply offered Denyse congratulations on her singing. Dozens and dozens of people introduced themselves to me and shook my hand. Were they just being friendly, or were they trying to follow the words of the sermon and extend a hand of friendship to a "brother"?

"Come on, this way," Denyse said as she took my hand for a second and pulled me toward the front of the church. "If we go out the front door it'll take forever. My family always goes out the side door. It isn't like we need to shake the pastor's hand, because we'll see him at home soon enough."

I followed Denyse and we found ourselves outside behind the church. We circled around until we came to the car. Jamar was already waiting, sitting in the front seat. He had his hat pulled down low over his eyes again and his tie was off and in a ball on the dashboard. Denyse's mother was standing beside the car, having a conversation with a small group of women. Denyse and I climbed into the back seat.

"Hopefully she won't be too long," Denyse said.

Almost on cue Mrs. Smith waved goodbye to the women and got into the car.

"So, Jamar," she asked, as she started the engine, "what did you think of your father's sermon today?"

"It was okay," he said, and shrugged.

She backed out of the parking spot. "And what was your favourite part?" There was something in her voice—a familiar sort of mother tone—that made me think this was more than just an innocent question.

He didn't answer right away.

"Well?" she asked.

"Definitely the part about Jesus."

"Ahhhh," she said, nodding her head. "So, the part about Jesus and the money-changers and how he threw them from the temple."

What was she talking about? He hadn't talked about that at all!

"Yeah, that's the part," Jamar agreed.

"Funny," Mrs. Smith said, "your father mentioned that story during the sermon *three weeks ago*."

"Oh," Jamar said. "I didn't understand. You wanted to know my favourite part of *this* week's sermon?"

"I already know your favourite part of this week's sermon," she said.

"You do?"

"Yes. Your favourite part was when you and your friends sneaked out the side door just before your father started speaking and spent the whole service outside in the parking lot," she said.

He didn't answer, and we drove along in silence for a while.

"What did you think of the service, Thomas?" Denyse's mother finally asked, to break the silence.

"You were right, it was different, really different from the services I usually go to."

"How was it different?" Denyse asked.

"There was the choir—"

"Your church doesn't have a choir?"

"Not like that! Our choir only seems to sing boring songs that are always off key. Your choir was amazing! And that band! I couldn't believe there was a band in the church! The music was incredible!"

"And your favourite part of the music was, of course, my solo … correct?" Denyse prompted.

"Of course," I answered, although I was thinking about the band.

"And what did you think of my husband's sermon?"

"That was probably the best sermon I've ever heard in my entire life," I said.

"Today?" Jamar asked.

"I can't believe that you thought this wasn't going to be a very good one," I said to Denyse.

"That's because that wasn't the one I heard him practising around the house all week," she answered.

"It wasn't," her mother confirmed. "He was up early writing it today after he read the paper."

"It was really good," I said.

"That was definitely one of his best," Denyse said. "Some of his sermons could be used to cure insomnia."

"Ain't that the truth," Jamar chipped in.

"Although you must have been feeling a little uneasy at the beginning," Denyse said.

"Uneasy? Why?" I asked, trying to pretend I didn't know the answer.

"I just know I wouldn't have wanted to be the only white face in that crowd," Denyse said.

"I wasn't the only person who was white."

Denyse gave me a look—a look that meant, *So who was counting the faces this time?*

"I did see Mrs. Granger and her baby in the service today," Denyse's mother said. "She was sitting in the back so she could go to the nursery if her baby fussed."

"So there was one other white face," Denyse said.

"Well, I guess there was her baby, too," I said.

"The father of the baby is black so the baby is black," Jamar said.

"But if it's her baby and she's white, wouldn't the baby be half white?" I asked.

"That's not the way it works," Jamar said. "If the baby is half black then it's all black."

"How can that be?" I questioned. "It has to be half white if the mother is white."

"That doesn't matter. If there's *any* black blood in somebody they're *black*," Jamar insisted.

"But—"

"But nothing!" Jamar snapped.

"Settle yourself down," their mother said. "It's just that the legislation, in the days when the races were separate, was pretty clear: if you had black blood you didn't have the rights of whites."

"Even if your father was the president of the United States," Jamar said.

I knew what he was talking about. Some pretty famous people, including one of the presidents, had fathered children with black women.

"But that was a long time ago," I argued.

"There aren't any race laws now, but people who look black still get treated differently," Jamar said. "And that's why if you're half black, you're all black."

"I wonder how that view would fit into your father's sermon today," Mrs. Smith mused.

"What exactly did he say in this sermon?" Jamar asked.

"You had to be there," his mother said. "Maybe you could ask your father to repeat it for you tonight. Sort of your own private performance."

"I think I'll pass on that. Can't you just tell me?" he pleaded.

"It was about a young black guy who was killed by the police yesterday," Denyse answered.

"Sounds like a fun story," he said.

"Not fun, but it made for a moving sermon," their mother said. "So, Thomas, our family always has a few people over after church for a meal. Would you like to join us?"

"Um ... I'd better check with my parents."

"It would be great if you could join us," Denyse said.

"And it would be quite a treat for my husband to meet somebody who thought his sermon was the best he'd ever heard."

"Can you check? Please?" Denyse slipped her hand over top of mine on the seat, and I knew where I was eating lunch.

THE FOOD WAS ALL SET OUT on the side-board. There were big bowls of potato and macaroni salad and rice, along with cold cuts and a gigantic platter of chicken wings. It looked and smelled great.

"Are you hungry?" Denyse asked as she carried out a large bowl brimming over with buns and bread.

"Definitely. But it would take an army to eat all of this!"

"I don't know about an army, but we might be feeding a lot of troops," she said.

"How many people are you expecting?"

"That's just it. We never know what to expect. It could be two or it could be twenty-two, depending on who my father invites."

"That reminds me, what do I call your father?" I asked.

"'Sir' is usually safe," she said, and laughed.

"I mean do I call him 'Mr. Smith' or 'Pastor Smith' or 'Reverend Smith'?"

"At church people call him 'Pastor.' Around here he usually gets—"

Denyse was interrupted by loud voices and laughter coming into the house. It sounded as

though a lot more than two people were coming
to lunch. Her father came into the room followed
by six older women, all decked out in fancy
dresses and big hats.

"And you must be young Thomas!" the pastor
said in a booming voice as he walked over and
shook my hand.

"Yes I am, sir. I really liked your sermon!" I
blurted out.

He burst into laughter—a big, full laugh that
filled the whole room. "In that case, it's an even
greater pleasure to meet you!"

Mrs. Smith came into the room carrying
more food. She greeted the women and then
came over and gave her husband a peck on the
cheek.

"Are these all our guests?" she asked.

"There are two more." He paused. "They're
out on the driveway shooting some hoops."

"Is it who I think it is?" she asked.

He nodded.

"Then I'd best hide the good silverware."

"Sharon!"

"I'm just joking, although you have to admit,
there's at least a whisper of truth to it."

*Who are these people?* I wondered.

"It's good to have faith," the pastor said. "Besides, they've been coming to church, so that makes them Christians."

"Well, I've been in a barn a few times in my life but that doesn't make me a cow."

"Would you rather they were here or on the streets?"

She hesitated. "Here. At least I know that they'll be getting one good meal."

"Not to mention some good influence. It does them good to spend time around our son," the pastor said.

"I'm sure it does," she agreed. "Although I'm a little more concerned about their influence on him. Now, lunch is ready so go and get the boys."

I sat down at the table. Denyse took a seat on one side of me and one of the church ladies sat on the other side. Two of the guys I'd seen at church hanging out with Jamar came in from the driveway and sat directly across from me. They were older than me. They wore a dozen chains around each of their necks, low-hanging pants, and matching glares that were aimed right at me. If I'd met these two guys on the street instead of around a dining-room table I would have been pretty scared. Actually, who was I kidding? I was a little bit scared.

Denyse's dad took a seat at the head of the table. That's where my dad liked to sit, too.

"Let us give thanks," he said. He reached out and took the hands of the people sitting on either side of him. Denyse took one of my hands and the church lady took the other. I was even more grateful to be sitting where I was.

"Dear Lord," he began.

I bowed my head and closed my eyes.

"We wish to give thanks for the good food, the good company, and the good friends, both old and new, who have joined us in our circle of faith."

Denyse gave my hand a little squeeze.

"We are truly blessed and feel safe in Your love."

He continued with the prayer, making mention of people I didn't know and how they needed God's help or blessing, and I started to think about what it would be like to have a father who was a minister. I knew that church every week and prayers at every meal would only be the start. I imagined it would involve phone calls at all hours of the night, visits from people in the congregation, weddings, funerals, and an expectation that you had to act a certain way all the time because people would be watching.

"Amen!" the pastor boomed, and I quickly mumbled "Amen" along with everybody else seated around the table. We released each other's hands. The hand Denyse had been holding felt sort of sweaty. Was that from me or from her, or from both of us?

"Okay, everybody, dig in, and remember, there's plenty more!" Mrs. Smith said.

We started eating. The food was good and I was hungry, which of course made it taste even better. The conversation was lively and loud and friendly. Friendly, except for the guys across the table. It was hard to believe that they could chew and scowl at me at the same time without choking on their food.

"Daddy," Denyse said sweetly, "Thomas isn't the only one who thought your sermon today was wonderful. I think it was one of your best."

"Thank you, darling. That means a lot coming from you."

"I wonder what she's after?" Jamar questioned under his breath, but loudly enough for everybody at the table to hear.

"You'd have thought it was great sermon too, Jamar," Denyse went on. "That is, if you had been sitting in the church instead of standing out in the parking lot."

Jamar's eyes grew wide and angry while the two boys stopped scowling and began snickering. Mr. Smith—Pastor Smith—sat up straighter in his seat. He didn't say anything, but I had a feeling that words would come later.

"And do you know what made the sermon so good for me?" Denyse continued. "It was because I know you so well, Daddy, and I know that those weren't just words but what you truly believe."

"That is God's truth," one of the church ladies agreed.

The angry expression on Pastor Smith's face was replaced by a look of pride. "I always try to preach from my heart."

"The words made me think of the way you've always welcomed my friends into this house," Denyse said.

"Your friends will always be welcome here," he agreed. "Especially the fine ones like your friend Thomas, here."

I almost felt myself begin to blush.

"Oh, Daddy, you don't understand. Thomas isn't just my friend," Denyse said.

"He isn't?" Pastor Smith asked.

"No." She shook her head. "He's my *boyfriend*," she said sweetly as she reached over and took my hand.

# *CHAPTER THIRTEEN*

I HAD THE STRANGE SENSATION that the laws of time and space had suddenly been suspended. The room seemed to have magically grown smaller, and time was standing still. I looked around the table from face to face. The only thing they all shared was their colour. There was a range of emotions on those faces: shock, surprise, pleasure, anger, and confusion. The anger was on Jamar's face. His two friends looked confused. Her father shocked. Her mother surprised. The church ladies all looked happy, as though they were genuinely pleased with what Denyse had announced. Why couldn't *they* have looked angry, shocked, and confused, while at least somebody in Denyse's family looked remotely happy?

"Excuse me?" her father questioned. "What did you just say?"

There was a pause, as though everybody in the place was collectively holding their breath, waiting for what might happen next. Maybe she would say something different, tell them it was all a big joke, or—

"I said that Thomas is not only my friend; he's my boyfriend."

There could be no doubt that Denyse's father had heard her—twice, now—but his facial expression remained unchanged. At most it went from surprised to shocked.

"You always said that when I had a boyfriend it would be important for me to bring him straight home to meet you, right?"

"Um … yes … yes," her father stammered. He didn't strike me as somebody who was often at a loss for words.

"So, Mom and Dad, this is my boyfriend, Thomas Martin," she said. She tightened her grip on my hand, but the way I was having trouble getting air into my lungs it felt more like somebody had their hands around my throat.

"Jamar," Pastor Smith said, "I would appreciate it
if you and your friends would excuse yourselves.
Perhaps you could go and play some basketball,
and we'll call you back in when dessert is served."

Without saying a word Jamar rose to his feet,
and his two friends did the same. But before he
turned to leave, Jamar gave me a look that could
only be described as pure and clean anger.

"Why don't we clean up?" one of the church
ladies suggested. She practically jumped to her
feet, and a split second later there was a scrap-
ing of chairs as the other five got up, and they
all grabbed plates and glasses and scurried
away into the kitchen. I was amazed by how
fast they moved. I wondered if I could jump
up and join them and hope nobody would
notice. But as I saw Denyse's father's eyes
aimed right at me, I knew that wasn't going to
be a possibility.

"When did all this happen?" her father asked.
"This boyfriend stuff?"

"I guess yesterday," Denyse answered.

I was so glad she'd spoken, because the lump in
my throat was getting bigger. And it felt like my
hand, underneath her hand, was practically on

fire. Was there any way I could discreetly slip it out from underneath hers?

"And just how long have you two known each other?" he asked.

"Since the start of the school year," Denyse answered.

I tried not to register surprise on my face. Maybe she'd known *of* me since then, but really we had met only nine days ago.

"So, *two whole months*," Pastor Smith said. "That long?"

"Didn't you and Mom know each other for about an hour when you first asked her out?" Denyse asked.

Nobody answered.

"You met at a church picnic," Denyse said, "and Mom's father was really protective and didn't like boys talking to her. Right, Mom?"

"He was a bit of a mother hen," she said.

"And then you two got talking when nobody was looking, and you asked her to go with you to a dance the next weekend, and she said yes, and she sneaked out without her father knowing and—"

"We're familiar with the story," her father said.

"And you told me that you hoped I never had to sneak off like that when I had my first boyfriend. So I didn't."

Her father let out a big sigh. "I see. And when your mother and I met, you are aware that I was seventeen and she was fifteen. Quite a bit older than the two of you."

"I know, and that's why I thought it was even more important that I not sneak around behind your backs," Denyse explained.

That certainly did make sense.

"And did you also feel that it was important to tell us in front of a large audience?" Denyse's mother asked.

"I guess I was just so moved by Dad's sermon that I wanted to share my commitment to his message," she offered.

Her mother's expression was very skeptical. I have to admit, that explanation sounded suspicious to me, too. I wondered if she'd made her announcement in front of everybody so that her parents wouldn't have a chance to get mad. Of course, now there was no audience except me.

"Perhaps we need to talk," her mother said.

"We are talking," Denyse offered.

"Privately. Thomas, would you excuse us so we can have a *discussion* with our daughter?"

"Sure, of course!" I exclaimed as I jumped to my feet. I was grateful to have an excuse to go somewhere—anywhere—else.

"No, I think he needs to be here," Denyse protested. She held on to my hand firmly, anchoring me to the table. "This is about the two of us, so you should talk to the two of us."

My mouth dropped open as my heart rose into my throat.

"I understand how you might think that," Mrs. Smith said, "but you're wrong." She turned to me. "This isn't about the two of you. It's about our daughter's decision to share this information in the way she did. Thomas, you can either go into the kitchen and help clean up or go out onto the driveway with the boys."

For a split second I thought that it might be better to go into the kitchen. Maybe I'd have to help with the dishes, but at least those women were friendly. Did I really want to be out there with the guys?

"At the front door there's a deacon's bench," Mrs. Smith said. "If you open it up you'll find dozens of pairs of basketball shoes. I'm sure at least one pair will fit you."

"Thanks," I said. Clearly, she expected me to play basketball with Jamar and his friends! How would that work out?

Denyse released my hand. I looked down at her and she gave me a very weak, scared little smile. I suddenly had the urge to stay—not because I wanted to be there, but because I didn't want her to face it alone—but I knew it wasn't my place. I reached back down and gave her hand a little squeeze.

"I'll be right outside if anybody wants to say anything to me," I said.

I listened as I walked away. I could hear voices, but they weren't loud or angry. That was good. At least, I *thought* it was good.

I stopped at the front door and opened up the deacon's bench. It was filled to the top and over-flowing with basketball shoes. There had to be dozens and dozens of pairs! All sorts of styles and types. Some were worn and beaten up, missing laces, but others looked as though they'd hardly been used. I dug in and grabbed a shoe that looked about right. I opened up the laces and looked for the size. It was too worn to read. I held it up to my dress shoe. It was almost identical. I searched through the pile until I found its match. Then I closed the deacon's bench, took a seat, and changed into them. It felt good to get out of my dressy leather shoes, and even better to slip into a pair of basketball shoes. I stood up and took a few steps. They fit almost perfectly, although they certainly didn't match my dress clothes. That left only one thing to do. I walked out the front door.

Jamar and his two friends didn't seem to be playing a game, they were just fooling around, taking shots at the net. I walked over and stood at the edge of the driveway, watching, not talking. They didn't seem to notice me. They were all trash-talking, making claims about who was best and who couldn't play at all. It wasn't much different from the things my friends and I said to each other all the time.

"Look what we've got here," one of the guys said. He came over to me, holding the basketball in one hand. "Do you play ball?"

"Yeah."

"And I bet you think you're pretty good, don't you?"

"I can play," I said. "I play rep ball."

"Rep?" He started to chuckle. "You mean you play for one of those teams from the suburbs where everybody has a fancy uniform and a warm-up jacket with their name on the back?"

Yeah, it did have my name on the back, as a matter of fact.

"Most of those kids don't know nothing about playing ball," he continued.

"You mean kids like Jamar?" I asked. "He plays for the same league I do."

"You two are teammates?" the other kid asked, incredulous.

"We're not on the same team!" Jamar exclaimed. "We both play for Monarch teams, but I play on the *midget* team. He plays *bantam*."

"Midget? Bantam? What the hell does that mean?" the first guy demanded.

"It means we're different ages," Jamar explained. "I'm two years older than him."

The one kid, the one standing right in front of me, got a thoughtful look on his face as he stared at me. "I didn't know how old he was. White kids all look young to me. How old are you, anyway?"

"I'm thirteen," I said.

"Same as me," he said.

"You're thirteen?" I figured he was at least a year, maybe two years older than me because he was so big—not just a few inches taller than me, also a lot heavier.

"Yeah. And my brother, LaRon, is fifteen."

"Your brother?"

"Yeah, that's my big brother."

LaRon was almost as tall as Jamar, and I figured him to be older as well.

"You didn't know we were brothers?" LaRon asked. "Most people think O'Ryan and I look practically identical." He paused. "But a whole lot of white people think that all black people look the same, so maybe that's your problem."

I had a problem, but that wasn't it. Now that they were standing side by side they did look the same: same angry scowl and bad attitude. What had I done to bring any of this on?

"So are we going to play a little ball?" the younger of the two, O'Ryan, asked.

"Why don't we just shoot around?" Jamar asked.

"That's boring," LaRon said. "We've got four players—well, at least four people," he said, shooting a glare my way, "so let's play a little two on two."

"What would be the teams?" Jamar asked.

"How about me and my brother," O'Ryan said, "against you and your brother."

"Maybe you mean him and his brother-in-law!" LaRon exclaimed.

"Funny, real funny," Jamar said. He didn't look too amused.

"I just hope you two don't beat on us too bad," LaRon said. "You know, 'cause you two are *rep* players and can call all sorts of cute little plays. You gotta promise not to beat us too bad. Promise?"

The two brothers started to laugh, and the younger one came over and gave his brother a low-five and a slap on the back.

"Unless you're too scared to play us?" O'Ryan asked.

Jamar stepped toward O'Ryan, and for a split second I thought he was going to take a swing at him. Instead he grabbed the ball and ripped it out of his hands.

"We get first ball, unless you're too scared to let us have it," Jamar said.

"That's no problem. You can have first ball, 'cause we're gonna have last ball ... the one I sink for the winning shot," LaRon bragged. "But I do see one problem. These two don't have their fancy uniforms on, so how can we tell the two teams apart?"

What was he talking about? There were only four of us, so who couldn't figure out who to pass the ball to?

"Maybe we could go skins and shirts," O'Ryan suggested.

"Oh, wait a second, I got another way we can tell the two teams apart. We're black and they're white," LaRon said.

"White?" I questioned. "My shirt is blue and Jamar's is ..." I stopped myself.

"Real funny," Jamar said. "You just keep shooting off your mouth and this is going to be more than just a basketball game." He walked out to the sidewalk and I hurried after him.

"Game is to ten points. Inside baskets are worth one point, shots from the three-point line count as two," Jamar said. "Cutthroat, so if you score you keep the ball. Steals or offensive rebounds have to be taken outside the three-point

line before they can be put back in. Call your own
fouls. Okay?"

"Don't matter what the rules are," LaRon said.
"You make the rules and we'll make the baskets."

"What do you want me to do?" I asked Jamar.

"I want you to start by getting rid of that
stupid tie."

I'd forgotten all about the fact that I was still
wearing my good clothes and a tie. I grabbed the
tie, pulled it off over my head, and threw it down
on the grass. I just hoped that I didn't rip up my
pants. I didn't really have many dress clothes, and
my mother wouldn't be happy if I ruined them.

"Do you want to run a play?" I asked.

"You inbound and then try to stay out of my way,"
he said. "It'll be hard enough to get around the two
of them without having to bump into you too."

I was going to say something, but what was the
point? Besides, did I really want to go under the
net with either of those two and bang around for
the ball?

"Check," I said, passing the ball to O'Ryan.

He whipped it back at me. If I hadn't had my
hands up it would have smashed me right in the
face. He smirked at me. I'd be ready the next time.

Jamar came across the front of the key with LaRon clinging to him. He spun to the side and doubled back. I bounced the pass around O'Ryan and into Jamar's hands. He put down his dribble, moved around LaRon, and broke in for the drive to the hoop. He laid the ball up and he was smashed from behind!

"Foul!" I screamed as the ball dropped in for a basket.

"No foul!" O'Ryan yelled back.

"He hit him from behind with both hands!"

"No foul!" LaRon protested. "He ain't bleeding so it's no foul!"

Jamar picked himself up. "No foul," he said. "Put the ball in."

I picked up the ball and tossed it to O'Ryan for a check. This time instead of whipping it back he slowly rolled it to me.

"I wanted to make sure you weren't going to complain that I tossed it too hard," he said.

"Nobody's complaining about anything," Jamar said. "Let's play ball."

He came right out to me, and LaRon came running right out with him. I knew what he was doing. At the instant Jamar stopped and started back toward the hoop I tossed the ball over his head, and he grabbed it and laid in an easy layup.

"Come on, man, you got to start playing!" O'Ryan yelled at his brother.

"You should have blocked the pass coming in!" he screamed back.

"You girls going to talk or play basketball?" Jamar asked.

LaRon said something under his breath that I couldn't hear but figured I understood anyway.

Jamar took the ball and tossed it to me. In turn I passed it to O'Ryan for the check. This time he walked away with the ball until he was right under the net. He then threw it back to me. They were going to make it impossible for us to make an easy layup. Jamar broke up toward me and I threw in the pass. Instantly LaRon was on him, reaching in for the ball. He slapped at Jamar, hitting him on the arm, reaching in, pushing and shoving, doing things that would have been a half-dozen fouls. O'Ryan was standing just behind his brother. Even if Jamar could get by him there was no way he was getting by the two of them.

I broke in for the hoop, uncovered. I raised up my hand and, seeing that Jamar had seen me break, I waited for the pass to come and ... he dribbled off to the side instead. Both LaRon and O'Ryan swarmed him, smacking at him and the ball until finally it popped free and LaRon grabbed it. Jamar had been fouled at least five times while they were getting the ball away from him but he hadn't called a foul. The only thing more confusing than that was why he hadn't passed to me for the easy basket.

LaRon took the ball outside of the three-point line. "Now you're going to see how it's done!"

Without a word Jamar went out on LaRon and I went to cover O'Ryan, who had planted himself under the hoop. He was taller and stronger than me so I tried to front him—stand between him and the ball. I backed in close and then, with a two-handed shove, I was sent sprawling forward, practically landing on my face. The ball sailed to O'Ryan, who put it in for an easy basket.

"That was a foul!" I screamed.

"No foul," Jamar said. "That wasn't a foul."

"Of course that was a foul!" I protested.

"I don't see no blood," LaRon said. "No blood, no foul."

Jamar walked back to me. "That was no foul.
Just play the game."

"That was a foul, and I *would* have played the
game if you'd passed me the ball when I was open!"

He scowled. "Just cover your man. You can't
play like some sort of girl! Don't let him push
you around!"

"Somebody gonna take the check?" O'Ryan
asked.

I walked out to him and he tossed the ball to
me. Without thinking I whipped it back at him,
deflecting off his hands and hitting him in the side
of the head.

"What's the idea!" he screamed as he jumped
toward me.

"The idea's that you should learn to catch!"
Jamar yelled as he stepped in between the two of
us. O'Ryan backed off.

O'Ryan picked up the ball and sent in a pass. It
deflected off one of my hands and Jamar snared
it. He instantly dribbled outside the line,
reversed, and started back in, with both players
covering him. I yelled for the ball and to my
surprise Jamar passed it out to me. I squared to
the net and sent up a long shot ... it dropped!

Jamar scooped up the loose ball and walked over and handed it to me. "Nice shot," he said under his breath. "That's a two ball," he said to the brothers.

I passed the ball to LaRon for the check, and he tossed it back to me. Without hesitating I tossed the ball in to Jamar before the two of them could get on top of him. To my surprise he threw it back to me. I set for the shot, put it up, and it dropped!

"That's another two!" Jamar yelled. "That makes it five to one!" Jamar picked up the ball. "I'll inbound the ball." He tossed it to LaRon for the check. He threw it back to Jamar.

I scrambled around trying to get free for the pass. O'Ryan stuck out his arms to corral me. As I broke, he hooked an arm around my arm, locking me in place, while I struggled to break away.

"Get open!" Jamar yelled.

I swung my arm around, trying to get free, and it came up and hit O'Ryan in the side of the head. He stumbled backward and I fell the other way as he released his hold on my arm. Jamar sent in the pass and I was able to reach over and grab it. Both LaRon and O'Ryan rushed at me and I tossed the ball back to Jamar. LaRon turned to chase Jamar but his brother simply kept coming, bowling me over. As I tumbled backward I saw Jamar put the ball in for another basket! I rose to my feet and brushed myself off. The pants were still in one piece but one of my hands was scraped up and bleeding slightly.

Jamar grabbed the loose ball and walked it back to the top of the key.

"Nice basket," I said.

"Nice pass. How about if you inbound this one?" Jamar asked as he handed me the ball. That did seem like a good idea.

I checked the ball with O'Ryan. Surprisingly he just tossed it back to me. He then went to help his brother cover Jamar. Jamar got the pass and immediately pitched it back outside. I put up the shot and it dropped again!

"That's nine to one!" Jamar yelled. "Next basket wins."

"We're getting the next basket, and the one after that, and the one after that!" LaRon snapped.

"Even if you got the next three we'd still win," I argued, amazed that I was talking back to this guy.

"How about you stop playing chicken ball and bring the ball down here into the paint!" he taunted.

"I've got baskets inside!" Jamar snapped.

"I'm not talking to you! I'm talking to that little girl!" he said, pointing at me.

"Some little girl," Jamar scoffed. "If he's a little girl and he's beating you, what does that make the two of you?"

"Where we come from, only little girls shoot from the outside! A *man* brings it down here into the paint, into the *house* … into *my* house!"

Jamar walked over to me. "If you can shoot, then shoot. Don't let him make you do something you don't want to do," he said under his breath. He handed me the ball and walked back toward the hoop. As he went, both of the brothers surrounded him. I tossed the ball into LaRon for the check. He threw it back out.

Jamar broke away from the net and I tossed the ball. Jamar jumped up and rather than grabbing the ball he bounced it right back to me. I squared for the shot as LaRon raced toward me, his hands up, trying to block the shot. I pump-faked as LaRon shot through the air and past me. O'Ryan charged toward me and I put a pass over for Jamar. I then broke for the net with my hand up in the air.

"Pass!" I screamed.

The ball came sailing over O'Ryan's head toward me. I grabbed it and laid it up and it went in the net for an easy basket and—I was bowled off my feet and landed in a heap beside the driveway!

I sat up. The knees were ripped out of both legs of my pants. My mother was going to kill me!

LaRon stood over top of me, scowling. "So was that a foul?" he taunted. "Was that a foul?"

I spat onto the driveway—spit was mixed with blood from the place where my teeth had been driven through my lip. I stood up.

"No foul," I said, "but that is game.

# *CHAPTER FOURTEEN*

"THAT MUST HURT SOMETHING AWFUL," Denyse's mother said as she tried to clean the cinders out of my leg. She was working on a spot just below the gash that Denyse had fixed up the week before.

Denyse and her father sat watching. Jamar was out on the driveway still shooting baskets. LaRon, O'Ryan, and the six church ladies had left.

"It hurts, but not as badly as the cuts on my mouth. They *really* hurt."

"How about your eye?" she asked.

"My eye?"

She reached over and touched the side of my face. I felt a shot of pain and recoiled from her touch.

"O'Ryan was hurt in almost the same place," she said.

"You two didn't punch each other, did you?" Pastor Smith asked.

"No, of course not! We were just playing basketball."

"Is that what you call it?" her mother asked. "I've heard of wars that didn't produce as many injuries. This isn't how I was expecting to be spending my Sunday afternoon."

"I can take care of the cuts, Mom," Denyse offered.

"I think you've done just about enough today," her father snapped.

What had Denyse done? It wasn't like she was the one who had bashed me around out on the court.

"You know that that boy has a crush on you," her mother said.

What boy was she talking about?

"I didn't know that," Denyse said. "Not for sure."

"And you announcing that Thomas was your boyfriend was like waving a red flag in front of a bull. How did you think O'Ryan was going to react?"

"O'Ryan has a crush on you?" I asked in amazement.

Denyse shrugged. "That's what my mother thinks."

"That's what all of us who have eyes think!" her father exclaimed. "Didn't you notice the way he was glaring at Thomas all through the meal?"

Of course I'd noticed, but I'd also seen the same glare on LaRon's face. Either they both had a crush on Denyse, or they both didn't like me for other reasons. And of course the only reason I could think of was the colour of my skin.

"I didn't notice him at all, and I don't care if he does have a crush on me!" Denyse replied. "He's a thug, and an idiot! Would you two be happier if he were my boyfriend?"

"You know we wouldn't be happy about that."

"Why not, he's black, so wouldn't that be *easier*?" Denyse demanded.

"Easier?" I asked.

Nobody answered right away. Her father looked away.

"My parents told me that—"

"What your parents told you is between them and you," her mother said quickly.

Denyse looked as though she was going to say something, but she didn't.

"Did your parents tell you it would be easier if I were black?" I asked.

Denyse looked to her father as though asking permission to answer. Instead, he said, "Thomas, you seem like a fine young man."

"He *is* a fine young man," Denyse said.

The pastor nodded in agreement. "And I'm sure most parents would be very pleased to have you as their daughter's boyfriend. But the fact that Denyse is black and you are white makes things much more—"

"Complicated," I said. "More difficult."

He nodded. "Yes, complicated and difficult."

"And what you want for your daughter is for things to be as easy as possible," I continued.

"Exactly!" Pastor Smith agreed. "That's exactly what we told Denyse!" He turned to his daughter. "You see, Denyse? Thomas agrees!"

"I didn't say I agree," I said.

"But, if you don't, then how could you use the exact words?" Mrs. Smith asked.

"Because those are the same words my father used when he talked to me this morning."

All three of them looked surprised.

"And your father thinks we shouldn't see each other?" Denyse asked.

"He didn't say that," I answered.

"And neither did we," her mother added.

"He just told me that things would be easier if you were white. He said that some people wouldn't understand, that they'd give us a hard time."

"People like O'Ryan," Denyse's mother said.

"You mean idiots like O'Ryan!" Denyse exclaimed. "You think I should let my life be dictated by a few morons like him?"

"First off, child, there are a whole lot more than a *few* people who think like him," her mother scolded her. "And second, nobody is saying you have to live your life according to the prejudices of others."

"Your parents just want you to have your eyes wide open," I said.

"Exactly! Didn't we tell you that?" her father said, nodding his head enthusiastically.

"Whose side are you on?" Denyse demanded of me.

"Your side, I mean, *our* side. I'm just saying what my father said to me."

"And it's starting to sound like you agree with him," Denyse snapped.

"I don't agree with most of what he said."

"But you agree with some of it?" she demanded.

"I do now."

"What do you agree with?" her father asked.

"The part about how some people are going to give us a hard time. Like O'Ryan today."

"Yeah, but maybe that didn't have anything to do with you being white," Denyse said. "Like you said, Mom, it could just be because he was jealous."

"But it was LaRon who ran me over at the end," I pointed out.

"And that might have been because he's a sore loser, right?"

I shrugged. "I guess it could have been."

"But you really don't know for sure, do you?" her mother asked.

"Well, no, not for sure," I admitted.

"And that's part of what we were talking to Denyse about," her father continued. "You just never know the reason behind how people react. It could be because of jealousy, or because he's a bad sport, or it could be because you're white."

"The thing is, you'll never really know," her mother added. "And that's what makes it so complicated."

"Complicated or not, we're not going to let other people dictate what we do or don't do. Right, Thomas?" Denyse asked.

"Right," I agreed, although at that moment, with the taste of blood still lingering in my mouth, my leg still stinging, and her parents standing over me, I didn't feel quite as sure as she seemed to.

"And you're saying that we are free to see each other, right?" she asked her parents.

"That's a decision for you and Thomas to make," her father agreed.

"Then it's settled," she said, defiantly.

I stood up. "I'd better be getting home."

"I feel so bad about your clothes being all torn," Denyse's mother said.

"That's okay."

"It just feels like somehow it was our fault. We shouldn't have sent you out to the driveway to play basketball."

"You couldn't have known what was going to happen," I assured her.

Neither of them answered, although both of them looked unsure of things.

"Maybe," her father said, "we should have seen this coming. In hindsight, perhaps we should have been able to predict what transpired."

"Do you want me to drive you home, or call your mother to explain things?" Mrs. Smith asked.

"I can walk, and it isn't like this is the first time I've ruined clothes playing basketball. I really have to go. Thanks for lunch, and for taking me to church."

"You are more than welcome," her father said. "It was our pleasure!"

"I'll walk you out," Denyse offered.

I followed her toward the door, but I stopped just as I was about to leave the kitchen and turned around. "I meant what I said about your sermon. It was really good."

"Thanks," Pastor Smith said.

I turned to walk away.

"Thomas?" he called out.

I stopped and spun back around.

"I meant what I said in that sermon. People have to reach out to their brothers, or prejudice wins."

I nodded. "Thanks."

Denyse came out the front door and walked me to the end of the driveway.

"So, do you still want to be my boyfriend?"

"Do you still want to be my girlfriend?"

She smiled. "Let me give you an answer this way." Denyse reached up to kiss me and I jumped away.

"What's wrong, don't you want me to kiss you?"

"Sorry, it's just that my mouth is hurting so much. We have to kiss really, really gently," I explained.

"I can do that, I think." Denyse placed her lips against mine ever so softly. Even softly, it still sent a buzz through my entire body that removed any doubts about wanting her for my girlfriend.

"How was that?" she asked.

"Nice. I guess we're lucky O'Ryan wasn't here to see that," I said.

"Or anybody like him." Denyse looked around. "If my parents are right, then black people are going to be mad at you and white people are going to be mad at me."

"Well, at least it's good to know that the Chinese are on our side, and there are *billions* of them."

Denyse laughed, and I laughed along with her. She reached up and gave me another gentle kiss.

"I'll see you tomorrow at school."

# CHAPTER FIFTEEN

"HEY, TOM, WAIT UP!"

I turned around to wait for Steve to catch up to me. Other kids, rushing to first-period classes, flowed around us.

"So how was—whoa, what happened to you?" Steve exclaimed.

"Lots of things. It was a busy weekend."

"I mean your face, of course."

My lower lip was all swollen and puffy, and the side of my right eye was coming up in a black and yellow bruise.

"Basketball injuries."

"Basketball? It looks like you were in a fistfight and somebody beat the crap out of you."

"Somebody did beat the crap out of me, but it was, in fact, during a basketball game."

"When did you play?"

"Yesterday, on Denyse's driveway."

"Were you playing with her brother?" Steve asked.

I nodded.

"And he did that to you?"

I'd told Steve about how Jamar felt about me.

"Actually, Jamar was on *my* side. We were playing against these brothers."

"'Brothers' like they were black guys, or 'brothers' like they have the same mother and father?"

"Same parents, but they were black, too. They live in the city."

"Two black guys from the city ... they must be really good players."

"They were okay," I said.

"Just okay?"

"We beat them ten to one."

"You did?" Steve sounded surprised.

"Do you think I'm lying?"

"No, of course not. I just figured that a couple of guys from the city—you know, black guys—"

"Just because a guy's black doesn't mean he can play basketball, you know!" I snapped.

"Well, you've got to admit that most of the players in the NBA are black," Steve said.

"Yeah, but that doesn't mean that all black players are better than all white players!" I protested. "Do you know how tired I get of having to prove to people that I can play basketball, because I'm white?"

"People don't think that," he said.

"*You* thought that!"

"I did not," Steve replied.

"Of course you did. You heard that these guys were black and you were surprised—shocked—that a team with me on it could beat them!"

Steve didn't answer.

"It's nothing but prejudice. Because I'm white, I can't play basketball or sing or dance!"

"But you *can't* dance," Steve said.

"Maybe I can't, but that isn't because I'm white, it's because I hate dancing!"

"Look, Tom, keep your voice down," Steve said. "Don't be mad at me."

"I'm not mad at you … well, not really mad at you."

"You should be mad at the guy who did all that damage to you. Did you at least give as good as you got?"

"I gave some," I said. "I smashed O'Ryan in the face really hard."

"O'Ryan? He sounds Irish," Steve said.

"That's his first name, not his last name. His brother was called LaRon."

Steve shook his head. "Sometimes I think Steven is boring, but I'll take boring over bizarre. Why do black people always have such strange names? What do they do, put all the letters of a Scrabble game into a hat and draw them out until they make a name?"

"Funny. Not all black people have strange names!" I snapped. "What's so strange about Denyse?"

"Nothing, although she spells it kind of funny. And her brother's name, Jamar, is a little on the weird side," Steve said.

"I think Jamar is an African name. Lots of African-Americans have African names. Besides, there's a lot of white people around here with pretty strange names."

"Like who?"

"How about Montana or Mercedes or Amethyst or Precious?" Those were four girls in our school. "Last time I checked, all four of them were white! Who the heck names their kids after a state or a car?" I demanded.

"You have to admit, if you're going to name your kid after a car, at least Mercedes is a pretty nice car. It would be different if you called your kid Ford or Volkswagen."

I couldn't help but laugh.

"Besides, you really should keep your voice down. Mercedes just walked by, and if she heard you making fun of her name she'd probably run you down. If her parents had known how big she was going to get they probably would have named her Mack Truck instead."

I burst out laughing again. "It's hard to stay mad at you, Steve."

"That's the plan. So, aside from all that, how did things go with you and Denyse?"

"Come on, we'd better get to class or we'll be late," I said. I turned and walked away. Steve scrambled along and caught up to me.

"That's okay, you can talk while we walk. So, come on, how are things between you two?"

"I don't know, probably about the same as between you and Bridget."

"Well, then I'm sorry to hear that."

"What do you mean?" I asked.

"Bridget told me to drop dead."

"Wow, that must be a new record. It's usually at least two weeks before a girl wants you dead."

He shrugged. "I guess I asked for this one."

"You *asked* her to tell you to drop dead?"

"Very funny. No, it's just that I told her I had to go out to lunch with my family on Sunday so I couldn't see her."

"And she was mad at you because of that?" I asked.

"Well ... she really didn't get mad until she bumped into me at the mall ... at lunchtime ... on Sunday ... with Kim."

"You jerk!"

"That's what Bridget called me before she said I should drop dead. And Kim expressed a similar opinion when she figured out what I'd done to Bridget."

We stopped at our lockers. I dialled the combination and tossed my pack into the bottom.

"Do you want me to ask Denyse to talk to Bridget?"

"Don't bother. I think it's time I took a break from girls."

"What?" I exclaimed, turning around to face him. "What did you say? Am I still talking to Steve, here?"

"You heard me. I think it's time that I took a break from girls."

"Yeah, right."

"No, I'm serious."

"The longest break I've seen you take since you started dating is the time between ending a relationship with one girl and finding the next," I said.

"Yeah! And when you think about it, what's the point? They all end badly." He paused. "Not that I'm saying *your* relationship will end badly." He paused again. "So tell me, what's it like to be with Denyse?"

I shrugged. "It's nice."

"Cool. And kissing her—you have kissed her again, haven't you?"

"Yeah."

"Good. I just want to know, what's it like to kiss her?"

"It's good, of course."

"I know it's good. Kissing is always good. But is it ... different?"

I shrugged. "I haven't really kissed that many girls, but every girl is different, aren't they?"

"I've kissed a lot, and most of them are pretty much the same, but I've never kissed a girl like Denyse."

Suddenly I understood what he was getting at. "You mean because she's black?"

"Of course. Is it different?"

I shook my head. "You know, Steve, of all the stupid things you've ever said to me—and there've been a lot—that is probably the stupidest."

"So you're saying it *isn't* any different?"

"That's what I'm saying."

"Well, that's not what Aaron told me." Aaron was Steve's nineteen-year-old brother.

"And he's dated a black girl?"

"No, but he told me that he'd heard *the darker the berry, the sweeter the juice.*"

"What?" I demanded. "Denyse is a *girl*, not a *berry*!"

"So you're saying she's not a good kisser?"

"She's a wonderful kisser, but that's got to do with her, not her colour!" I snapped.

I realized that a whole bunch of eyes and ears were focused on us. Other kids walking by or standing at their lockers were staring.

"I was just thinking ... " Steve said.

"That would be a first," I muttered under my breath.

"I was thinking that maybe my problem with girls isn't about girls in general but about the specific girls I choose. Do you think that you could talk to Denyse for me? Maybe she could set me up with a nice black girl and I could find out about this kissing thing for myself."

"Haven't you been listening to anything I've said?"

"I've been listening to all of it. That doesn't mean I believe any of it. So, will you talk to her?"

I slammed my locker closed and locked it. "I'm not going to talk to her for you. And if you don't smarten up, I'm not going to talk to you about *her*. Got it?"

"Okay, all right already, I got it. Jeez, there's nothing like being too sensitive. Let's just forget we even talked and get to class."

That was probably the most sensible thing he'd said in a long time.

I HADN'T SEEN DENYSE all morning, but I knew I'd be able to find her at lunch in the cafeteria. That presented a slight problem, though. I wanted to eat lunch with both her and Steve, but I saw Bridget sitting with Denyse and I knew that Steve wasn't going to be welcome at that table. The only solution seemed to be to invite Denyse to eat lunch at my table, with the grade eights. That way, if she said no, then it would be her fault and not mine.

Steve and I worked our way across the cafeteria.

"I'm going to see Denyse. Do you want to come?"

"And talk to Bridget? Not likely."

"Then I'll meet you at our table," I said.

"Sure you will."

"I will! Here, take my lunch bag with you."

"You're trusting me with your lunch?"

He was right, that didn't seem too bright. "Just don't eat it all, okay?"

"That I can promise. Your mother always puts in healthy stuff that I wouldn't touch."

Steve walked over to join the rest of the guys and I headed toward Denyse. She saw me coming and gave me a big wave and a smile. She stood up and came toward me.

"Oh, my goodness … your face!"

"It's not as bad as it looks."

"Good, because it looks really awful!"

"Gee, thanks."

"It just looks so much worse than yesterday. Does it hurt?"

"Not too much."

"I'm glad. Come," she said as she took my hand, "join us for lunch."

I let her tow me along. "I can't."

She stopped and turned around. "Why not?"

"I think I should sit with Steve. He's pretty broken up about what happened between him and Bridget."

"He should be broken up—into little pieces. That was really a crummy thing he did. He really hurt my friend."

"He wasn't trying to hurt her."

"Well he did. That was awful."

"It was kind of lousy, for sure, but—"

"You're not going to defend him, are you?" she demanded.

"I'm not defending anybody!" I snapped.

"It certainly sounded like you were about to. If you don't think what he did was so bad, should

I expect to run into you at the mall with somebody else?"

"No, of course not, but that's different!"

"How is it different?"

"For one thing, we're going out and they
weren't."

"Well ... "

"And second, that's Steve and Bridget, not you
and me. You're not Bridget and I'm not Steve."

She didn't answer. That was a good thing.

"Right?"

"I guess so," she reluctantly admitted.

"Good. Now, would you like to come and join
me for lunch?"

"I'd like to, but I'd better stay with Bridget.
She's pretty upset."

"I understand."

"Besides, I'll see you after school."

"After school?" I asked.

"The game ... you are staying to watch me
play, right?"

Right, she'd mentioned yesterday that she was
playing after school and that I could watch "if I
wanted." I now knew that that wasn't just an open
invitation. Not coming would be like going away

and leaving her on the ski slopes when I wasn't supposed to.

"Of course I'm going to watch," I said. "I wouldn't miss it."

I could tell by her expression that I'd said the right thing. Now I'd have to call my mother and hope she could drive us home afterwards. Maybe I could even convince Steve to stay—that would make for an interesting drive home, with him and Denyse in the car together.

"So, I'll see you at the game," Denyse said.

"I'll be there."

Denyse moved close, got on her tiptoes, and gave me a kiss. I heard a loud gasp, then a few giggles, and a few laughs from the guys. I opened my eyes. It seemed as though everybody was staring at us. Some looked surprised and others just looked amused. What, they'd never seen a girl kiss her boyfriend before? Well, maybe not at lunch in the school cafeteria ...

"I thought a kiss might be a good idea," she said. "To sort of make up after our first fight."

"That wasn't much of a fight."

"As much as I ever want to have. I'll see you after school."

I stood there stunned, watching Denyse walk away ... boy, she walked away good.

"Way to go, Tom."

I looked over. It was my friend Nathan.

"Um ... thanks," I mumbled.

I started to walk away, and as I passed by, Nathan reached out and gave me a low-five. He wasn't mad about me being with Denyse, and he was black. Maybe not *all* black guys were going to be mad at me. Maybe it was only the ones who were jerks.

I hurried over to join my friends. I had twenty minutes to eat, convince Steve to stay after school, and call my mother to arrange a ride home afterwards.

# CHAPTER SIXTEEN

"THIS TIME YOU REALLY OWE ME," Steve said.

We settled into the first row of the bleachers.

"You're right, this time you are doing something for me because of a girl. The other two hundred and fifty-seven times it was me doing you a favour."

"Okay," Steve said, "I guess that makes us even."

"Even! How do you figure that makes us even?"

"Fine, so we're not even. But this might just work out my way, anyway."

"Do you think you still have a chance with Kim?" She was warming up on the court with the other girls.

"Not likely. I have somebody else in mind," Steve said.

"Who?" I scanned the girls warming up on the court with Denyse.

"Nobody from our team."

Then I turned and looked at the few kids sitting with us in the bleachers. I didn't see any likely candidates.

"You're looking in the wrong direction," Steve said. "She's on the court ... on the other team."

"The other team!"

"Yeah. I figure it's time I expanded my horizons and tried other schools."

"Is that because you've run out of girls at our school who will still talk to you?"

"Not likely. Can you tell who I've got my eye on?"

I hadn't been paying any attention to the other team at all. I looked over. There were twelve of them, and they were going through a layup drill. There were a couple of girls I immediately disqualified, knowing Steve. One was sort of chubby and another was really, really tall.

"Well, have you figured it out?"

"I'm working on it." Knowing Steve the way I did I figured this wouldn't be too difficult. I'd just pick out the girl who was blondest and skinniest—although there really wasn't anybody on the team who fit that description.

"Want me to tell you?" Steve asked.

"Sure."

"Number twelve."

I tried to pick out number twelve, but the number wasn't jumping out at me.

"She's going in for the layup now."

"Her?" I exclaimed. Then I suddenly remembered what Steve had said to me about changing the type of girl he was interested in.

"Why not her?" Steve asked.

"No reason. I just don't think you should try to go out with somebody simply because she's black."

"You think you're the only one who can date somebody who's black?"

"No, of course not. It's just that you don't ever go after white girls unless they have blond hair."

"I think that's my problem. I've been going after the wrong type of girls."

"So you think you should be dating only *black* girls?" I questioned.

"Black girls, girls with black hair, girls with red hair. Non-blondes, that's the point. What do you think about that?"

"I figure it can't work any worse than what you've been doing up to now. So, how are you going to meet her?"

"I was hoping you could help me there," Steve said.

"Me? You want me to go and talk to her?" I exclaimed.

"Of course not. I was hoping you'd get Denyse to introduce her to me."

"Denyse?" I said. "That girl is on the other team ... she goes to another school."

"I know that. I'm not stupid, you know."

I stifled the urge to argue with that last statement.

"It's just that Denyse is black and number twelve is black, so I figured she could go up and talk to her," he said.

"What, you figure that every black person knows every other black person?"

"I know she probably doesn't *know* her, but she could still go and talk to her. You know, go up and say something like, 'Hey girlfriend, you wanna meet my old man's main man?' or something like that."

"Steve, that is so ridiculous! I'm not going to ask Denyse to do that."

"Why not?"

"Because … I'm just not," I said.

"Then how do you expect me to get to know her?" Steve asked.

"I don't know. Wave to her or something."

"Wave?"

"Yeah, you know, put your hand up in the air and twirl it all around. You've probably seen it done in the movies."

"If that isn't the stupidest idea I've ever heard!"

"No stupider than thinking that Denyse could go over and talk to her just because she's—" I stopped as a ball bounced over toward me. I jumped up and grabbed it.

"Can I have my ball back?" Denyse asked as she jogged over toward me.

"Maybe."

She took the ball from my hands. "This is going to be a tough game."

"They don't look so tough."

"They're in first place. They haven't lost a game all season," she said.

"Ask her!" Steve called out from behind me. I tried to ignore him.

"Ask me what?" Denyse asked.

"I was wondering how you were going to get home after the game. I couldn't get a hold of my mother and I wondered if you were taking the bus or—"

"My mother's coming to pick me up. There's enough room in the car for you and Steve." She paused. "Steve doesn't want me to drive Kim home too, does he? Because I like her, but I couldn't do that to Bridget, and—"

"Don't worry about that," I said. "I think Kim and Bridget have the same opinion of Steve right now. Besides, he has his eye on somebody else. Somebody on the other team."

"He does?"

I nodded. "Number twelve."

"Kendra?"

"Kendra? You know her?"

Steve shot me an "I told you so" look. I wanted to reach over and give him a slap.

"We played on the same rep team a couple of years ago."

"Do you know any of the other girls on that team?" I asked. Three other girls on the team were black. Steve couldn't be right, could he?

"Nobody else."

I looked at Steve again, and this time I smirked.

Steve came over to join the conversation. "Any chance you could introduce the two of us?" he asked.

"I'm not going to introduce you to anybody," Denyse said. "After what you did to Bridget, I'm not going to help you meet anybody else."

"Fine with me," I said. "You'd better get back to the warm-ups."

"Right."

Denyse came forward and we kissed. Instead of a little peck, I held on to her for a few more seconds. I didn't know whether kissing talent had anything to do with skin colour, but she really was a good kisser.

"Wish me luck," she said.

"You don't need luck because you've got skill. Have a good game."

Denyse walked back across the court and I sat down.

"That wasn't very helpful," Steve said.

"She wasn't trying to be helpful. Try that waving thing I mentioned if you want to get her attention."

"I think kissing Denyse would work better," he said.

"What are you talking about?"

"When you and Denyse kissed, a whole bunch of girls on the other team stopped and watched, including number twelve. Denyse said her name was Kendra, right?"

I nodded.

"Good. Having her name is a place to start. I'll go and talk to her after the game ... she'll be happier then."

"Why do you think that?"

"Because people on the winning team are always happy."

"So now you're cheering for the other team?"

"Not necessarily. I just think they're going to win."

"Why? Wait, let me guess. You counted the number of black players on each side and figured, because they have four and our team only has two, they're going to win. You didn't do that, did you? Tell me you didn't do that."

"Well … that was part of it."

"And what was the rest of it?"

"I have been watching the other team's warm-ups. They just look stronger."

"I'll bet you Denyse is better than any of them."

"Spoken like a true boyfriend. I guess we'll find out soon enough."

The girls were coming up to centre court for the tip. Denyse was up against Kendra. They nodded as they came together. Kendra's expression didn't seem too friendly. Denyse had a scowl on her face. Then again, if I were playing against even my best friend—against Steve—it would have looked like I hated him, too.

The ball went up and Denyse and Kendra jumped. The ball bounced off their fingertips and over to a player from Kendra's team. That wasn't the greatest way to start, but the game had a long time to go.

The other team's point guard took the ball up the court. Kendra, who was obviously the team's centre, took up a spot in the low post. Denyse was a lot shorter but she was covering her. She fronted her to try to prevent the ball from coming inside. She and Kendra jostled and pushed and shoved for position. Whoever thinks that girls' basketball isn't physical never saw two players go at it the way those two were battling.

The ball went up. It was a long shot, and the ball bounced off the rim and sailed away from the hoop. Denyse jumped up, grabbed the ball with both hands, and was suddenly shoved through the air, sprawling face first onto the floor. Kendra had given her a two-handed shove to the back! The ref signalled the foul. She would have had to be totally blind to have missed that one.

"That was some shot," Steve said.

"She missed it."

"I didn't mean with the basketball. I meant the shot against Denyse's back."

Denyse picked herself up. She was still holding the ball. Even after being fouled hard she hadn't been willing to surrender the ball. That was so Denyse. If Kendra's plan was to intimidate Denyse to put her off her game she really didn't know her very well. That would only make Denyse more intense, and she'd play even better.

Our team took possession of the ball and tossed an inbound pass. Denyse took the ball up the court. She passed off to the centre and broke down the lane. I knew what was coming. She went backdoor and the pass came back and she went to lay it up and she was shoved into the wall, slamming against it and landing on the floor! Before I could even open my mouth to react, Denyse jumped back to her feet and started yelling at the player who'd pushed her. It wasn't Kendra, it was another girl. The ref stepped in between the two players. She signalled for a flagrant foul—that meant two shots—and we got the ball back.

"Is their plan to kill Denyse?" Steve asked.

"Maybe not kill her, but rough her up enough to get her so frustrated and angry that she won't be able to concentrate on her game."

Denyse put up the first foul shot and it dropped for a basket.

"They're going to find out that isn't going to work," I said.

She put up a second shot and it hit the front of the rim and clanged off to the side. No basket, but at least our team got the ball back. Our centre took the ball out of bounds and looked for Denyse to get free. Denyse spun and twisted and turned but it looked as though she and Kendra were all tangled up together and—the ref signalled another foul! Great, if they kept this up they'd all be fouled out before—what was that? I stood up, shocked at the ref's call: a double foul, one to Kendra and one to Denyse.

This was going to be one long, nasty game.

THE CLOCK SHOWED just over one minute left to play and the score was twenty-nine to twenty for our team. It had been a terrible game to watch. Three players on the other team, including Kendra, had fouled out. Denyse was only one foul away from being gone.

There had been more screaming and yelling between the players than in any other game I'd ever seen outside of the pros. The ref, who was probably some gym teacher from another school, was overwhelmed and out of her league in dealing with it. If I'd been her I would have tossed some people out—some people on the other team. There were four players on Kendra's team who seemed to have spent the entire game slapping and shoving and fouling Denyse. At least three of them were gone. It was beginning to look less as though they were trying to throw her off her game and more as though they were really trying to hurt her. Actually, it looked to me as though they were more interested in hurting Denyse than they were in winning the game. For the first time in my life I understood why sometimes during a game my mother would get up and leave the gym. There were more than a few times when it was just too hard to watch ... to see Denyse being hurt, knowing there was nothing I could do about it.

Of course, Denyse was no passive victim. A couple of times she'd come right back at them, shoving and screaming, and once I'd thought she was going to get into a fistfight right there in the middle of the floor in the middle of the game. I guess, in all fairness, if there had been a good ref Denyse would have been tossed out as well.

Now all I wanted was for the game to end uneventfully. This game was won, so I didn't know why Denyse was still on the floor. Then again, knowing Denyse, she probably wanted to stay out there to make a statement. Something like, "I survived, and even won the game."

Denyse had the ball and stood almost at half court, dribbling the ball, waiting for the game to end, the last few seconds ticking down. The buzzer sounded and both Steve and I jumped to our feet, along with the other spectators, and cheered. The two teams lined up at centre to shake hands. Denyse moved through the line. When she got to Kendra they both withdrew their hands, walking past each other. Denyse shook hands with the player behind Kendra and the one behind her and then pulled back her hand for the last three girls.

"Did you see that?" Steve asked.

"It was hard to miss."

"She wouldn't shake hands with four of the girls," Steve said. "The four black girls."

"They were the ones giving her the hard time," I said. "I don't know if I would have shaken hands with them either."

"I'm not so sure myself," Steve said. "I just know it looked pretty strange. Let's go over and congratulate them."

We started toward the bench, but there was some sort of meeting going on. The coach stood in the centre of the small crowd of players. They all looked very serious. These were not the sort of expressions I expected to see on the faces of a winning team.

"Let's just wait for them to finish," I said to Steve as I took him by the arm and slowed him down. "It would be better to wait here." Steve didn't argue.

We watched from a safe distance as they continued to talk. Denyse glanced over at me. She looked upset—very upset.

"What happened to Denyse?" Steve asked.

"What do you mean?" I asked, and then the answer became obvious. On the side of her arm there were three red gashes.

"It looks like she got cut."

"Looks more like scratches to me," Steve said. "It looks like she was in a cat fight."

He was right, they did look like scratches. I'd had a few swipes torn out of me over the years playing ball, but nothing like that.

The meeting broke up and Denyse looked over at me again. She looked upset ... like she was on the verge of crying. She came over.

"Your arm ... are you okay?" I asked.

"Yeah ... I'm ... I'm ... okay."

It was obvious that she was battling back tears that were starting to glisten in the corners of her eyes. Those scratches probably hurt like crazy, but that wouldn't be why.

"I have to get changed," she said.

"Are you sure you're okay?"

She burst into tears and ran away. Before I could even think how to react, she disappeared into the girls' change room.

# CHAPTER SEVENTEEN

"WHAT DO I DO NOW?" I asked Steve.

He shrugged and shook his head. "I don't know. *You* didn't do anything."

"Should I go after her?"

"Into the girls' change room?"

"Oh, yeah, right. Maybe I could send somebody in there to see if she's okay."

"You could send me, but that probably wouldn't work. Anyway, isn't the whole team in there now?"

He was right.

"I just want to make sure she's all right."

"Is she driving home with us?" Steve asked.

"Actually, we're driving home with her. Denyse's mother is coming to pick us up."

"Then you'll find out on the way home. Don't worry, she's probably just upset because of how rough the game was. You know how girls are."

"I don't know *anything* about girls," I said.

"Neither do I," Steve admitted, "but it sure is fun trying to figure it out."

"This is fun?" I asked.

"Maybe 'fun' isn't the right word ... but interesting, definitely interesting."

Denyse's mother came in through the doors at the far end of the gym. She looked around for her daughter. I waved. She saw me, waved back, and headed over.

"There's our ride," I said.

"Hello, Thomas. I guess I missed the end of the game. Did we win?"

"Yeah, by nine points," I said.

"So it was a good game."

"I don't know if I'd use that word," Steve said.

"This is my friend, Steve," I said.

"Nice to meet you," she said, "I'm Mrs. Smith," and they shook hands. "So, it *wasn't* a good game?"

"The result was good, but the game itself ..."

She gave me a questioning look.

"Denyse got hurt."

Her mother shook her head. "Nothing unusual there. That girl plays hard."

"Actually," Steve said, "it was more like somebody hurt her. Maybe on purpose."

"What happened?" Now she sounded anxious.

"It's her arm," I said. "She got scratched on the arm."

"And maybe her head is a little sore. She got smacked into the wall once and knocked down a couple of times," Steve added.

"That sounds awful. Were other players injured?"

I shook my head. "I don't think so ... at least not on our team."

"They were only picking on Denyse?" her mother asked.

"I think that was the other team's strategy. Since she's the best player on the team—"

"By *far* the best player on the team," Steve added.

"Yeah, by a lot. So they were after her all game."

"I've seen that happen to Jamar on more than a few occasions. It's hard to sit there and watch one of your children being hacked and smacked."

"It was hard for me, too," I agreed.

"But she's okay, just a few scratches and maybe some bruises, but nothing's broken or anything," Steve said, trying to sound reassuring.

"But she was really upset," I added.

"She was probably mad as a wet cat," her mother said.

"She was mad during the game, but after the game she was ... she was ..." Maybe I shouldn't have been saying anything.

"She was what?" her mother asked.

"I don't know."

"She was crying," Steve said.

"Denyse?" her mother asked. "*My* daughter?"

"Maybe it was just because her arm was hurting pretty bad. She really got raked over."

"I'd better go into the dressing room and have a—" She stopped as the team, including Denyse, came out of the change room.

"How are you, darling?" her mother asked.

"I'm okay."

"Are you sure?"

"Yes, I'm sure," she said, sounding annoyed. "Can Thomas come over for a while?"

"For a while, before supper."

"And can we give Steve a ride home? He lives a few blocks away on Coulter."

"That's not a problem."

"Good," Denyse said. Then she turned and walked away, leaving her mother, Steve, and me standing there. We scrambled after her, but she was moving quickly. By the time we got to the gym door she was already down the hall and halfway to the door leading to the parking lot.

As I stepped out the door I heard a low rumbling of music. Denyse, still well ahead of us, opened up the back door of the car to climb in and the sound swelled. It was coming from their car! Then I noticed Jamar in his customary spot, slumped in the front passenger seat. As we got closer, the loud, low bass sound was so strong that it almost made the car shake.

"I don't know how he can stand that so loud," Denyse's mother said.

"With some music, louder is better," Steve said.

"This is music?" she asked sarcastically.

Mrs. Smith went to the driver's door and pounded on the window. Jamar reached over and turned the music down. We all climbed in, Steve and me in the back with Denyse. Mrs. Smith turned the music down even more.

"Hey, I can hardly hear it now," Jamar protested.

"I've heard the lyrics to this one, and I think we'd all be better off if we couldn't hear a word," she snapped.

"This band isn't so bad," Steve said.

Jamar turned around and looked at Steve. "I hope this one isn't coming home with us, too."

"We are giving both of your sister's friends a ride to their homes," Mrs. Smith said.

"I guess there's no problem with us taking him to *his* home," Jamar said under his breath.

Mrs. Smith started the car and the sound of the engine drowned out the music completely. Jamar reached over and turned it up slightly.

"Thanks," Steve said. "This is one of my favourites."

"You like this song?" Jamar asked.

"Yeah, it has great lyrics and a great beat."

Jamar snorted. "I don't know what it is, but it seems like all the little white boys in the suburbs just *love* rap music."

"So, why should they be any different from all the little *black* boys in the suburbs?" Denyse asked. "It's not like anybody out here is so *street*, no matter how hard they pretend."

I could see Jamar straighten up in his seat and the muscles in the back of his neck tighten.

"Most of the kids who listen to all these rap tracks are suburban kids. White, black, or yellow, they're all just a bunch of posers pretending they're something they're not," Denyse continued.

"Look who's mouthing off about pretending to be something that she's not!" Jamar snapped.

"What does that mean?" Denyse protested.

"It means that you're the one——"

"Both of you stop it, now!" their mother yelled. "I won't have the two of you fighting, or I'm going to stop the car and you can both walk home!"

I glanced over at Denyse. I thought she'd be angry. Instead, she looked as though she was going to cry again.

"Tom, how is your face feeling?" Mrs. Smith asked.

"It looks worse than it feels," I said.

Jamar turned around in his seat and studied my face. "Good, 'cause I don't know how that could possibly *feel* any worse than it *looks*!"

Steve burst out laughing, and Jamar smiled.

"Did your friend tell you about our game on Sunday?" Jamar asked Steve.

"He told me a little about it."

"Rough game. Did you know he gave O'Ryan a black eye, too?" Jamar turned to me. "On that play when you two were all tangled and you smacked him in the face."

"Way to go, Tom!" Steve said.

"Of course," Jamar said, "with him, a black eye doesn't show quite as bad as it does on you."

"If you want to see rough, you should have seen your sister's game today," Steve said. "It was brutal!"

Jamar looked at Denyse. She stared straight ahead, not looking at him. She was fighting desperately not to cry.

Mrs. Smith turned the car onto Coulter Crescent.

"My house is just up ahead, with the green van parked in the driveway," Steve said. She stopped the car. "Thanks for the ride. Feel better,

Denyse!" He jumped out and slammed the door closed. We started off again.

"So where did you get hurt?" Jamar asked.

Denyse didn't answer, but I could tell that the tears were just below the surface.

"She got scratched on the arm," I said.

"Big deal. People get scratched all the time."

"And knocked down, and pushed into the wall once," I added, trying to defend her.

"Nothing broken, is there?" Jamar asked.

"Luckily," I replied.

"Then I don't see what the big deal is all about," he said.

"Jamar, you leave your sister alone!" their mother said.

"What? You play basketball, you get hurt. That's just the way of the game. Certainly nothing to *cry* about."

"Jamar, I'm warning you to——"

"I'm not crying!" Denyse exclaimed. "I'm just upset."

"So they pushed you around a little," Jamar went on. "You make sure you push them harder the next game. No need to get so upset."

"I'm not upset about what they did," Denyse said.

Everybody held their breath, waiting for her to explain what she meant.

"I'm upset about ... " Her voice was barely above a whisper.

"Upset about what?" her mother asked as we pulled into their driveway and the car came to a stop.

Denyse didn't answer. She burst into tears, jumped out of the car, and ran for the house.

# CHAPTER EIGHTEEN

MRS. SMITH JUMPED OUT OF THE CAR and raced after her daughter into the house. I sat there, too stunned to move, not sure what to do. Jamar got out of the car then, and that set me in motion. I climbed out too.

"Who was giving her a hard time in the game?" Jamar asked.

"Some of the players on the other team."

"Yeah, I figured it wasn't the players on *her* team, idiot. Which players on the other team?"

"I don't know exactly. There were three or four of them. One was named Kendra."

"The name doesn't mean anything to me. Were they black or white?"

"They were black ... mostly ... I guess."

"You guess? Were they black or not? You telling me that you don't know the difference?" he demanded.

"Okay, they were black."

"And before the game, were you two doing anything together? You know, like holding hands?" Jamar asked.

"Not holding hands," I said reluctantly. "But she did give me a kiss."

"Great," Jamar said.

He started for the house and I rushed after him. I grabbed him by the arm and turned him around.

"So what if she kissed me? So what?"

He shook his head and scowled. "Even if you two are different colours you're perfect for each other ... you're both equally *stupid*!" He tried to shake off my grip, but I held on.

"What do you mean?" I demanded. "What was so wrong about us kissing?"

"Just come on, let's see if Denyse is okay."

I let go of his arm and followed him into the house. As soon as we stepped in the door I could hear the sound of sobbing—Denyse crying. We followed the sound down the hall and into the living room. Denyse was slouched over on the sofa, her face buried in her mother's shoulder, their arms wrapped around each other. Jamar walked over and put a hand on his sister's shoulder. I stood there, helpless, not feeling right about being there, but not able to leave——not *wanting* to leave.

Slowly, gradually, the sobbing started to subside, and then there were just tears, and finally, after what seemed like an incredibly long time, there was silence.

Denyse and her mother looked up at me, and I felt kind of embarrassed to be there.

"I just wanted to make sure you were okay ... maybe I should go home," I said.

Denyse shook her head. "No ... stay ... please."

I didn't know what to say.

"You should stay," Denyse's mother said. "It does involve you."

I didn't know how exactly, but I knew she was right. Whatever had happened out there on the court had something to do with me——something to do with me being white.

Jamar dropped to a knee and placed a hand on his sister's shoulder. "What did those girls say to you?"

She raised her head, and she looked as though she was about to say something, but instead she began to sob again.

"You think she's crying because somebody said something to her?" her mother asked.

"It was some of the players on the other team, I think," Jamar said.

Mrs. Smith looked confused. "Denyse, is that true?"

Denyse nodded her head and tried to say something, but only sobs came out.

"So you're not hurt—physically—nothing's broken, right?"

Again Denyse nodded.

"Whatever did they say to you that got you so worked up?"

Denyse took a deep breath, gasped, and shuddered. She was trying to hold back the tears long enough to answer. "They … they said … that I … that I was an Oreo."

"What does that mean?" I questioned.

Jamar turned to me. "Figure it out, genius—a cookie that's black on the outside and white on the inside."

"They said they were going to … going to knock me around to see if they could … could make the white leak out," Denyse said. She began to sob again.

"Tell me the names of these people and I'll call their school and—"

"No!" Denyse exclaimed.

"But surely in this day and age we shouldn't have to put up with things like that happening!" their mother said.

Jamar scoffed. "They happen all the time."

"They said that I thought I was too good to go out with a black guy ... that I was being uppity."

Mrs. Smith shook her head sadly. "How would they even know that Thomas was your friend?"

"Because these two are so stupid that they kissed in front of everybody before the game!" Jamar snapped.

"We're not stupid!" Denyse protested.

"You are if you think you can do something like that without at least the possibility of somebody getting mad at you!" Jamar insisted.

"He's my boyfriend, and I can kiss him if I want!"

"If you want to risk being hassled!" Jamar said.

"But how could one kiss cause that much of a hassle?" I asked, stepping forward.

Jamar stood up and came toward me threaten-
ingly. "What don't you get? You're white and she's
black! People are going to make it a problem!"

I wanted to say something, to argue with him,
but I didn't. I couldn't. I'd been there, watching
the game, seeing with my own eyes how those
girls treated Denyse. Denyse took another deep
breath. I could tell she was fighting hard to keep
herself from sobbing again. She wiped her eyes
with the back of her hand.

"I think we could all use something to drink,"
Mrs. Smith said. She gave Denyse a little
squeeze around the shoulders and stood up. She
walked away to the kitchen, leaving Jamar,
Denyse, and me.

Denyse was still sitting on the couch, sniffling,
her eyes fixed on the floor. Jamar was now standing over his sister. It seemed almost like he was
guarding her. Maybe I should have been the one
guarding her, or at least offering to comfort her.
Maybe I should have figured out what was happening on that gym floor and done something about
it. But what? It wasn't like I could have run out
onto the court and yelled at those girls. There was
nothing I could have done, even if I'd understood

what was going on. I didn't know if I could bear to watch another one of her games ... but maybe it would be okay if I *didn't* come to any more games ... maybe it would even be better. If I hadn't been there, none of this would have happened. Or maybe we shouldn't have kissed. We probably shouldn't be doing that any more, kissing in a place where people could see us. And that meant that we shouldn't hold hands, either. That was the only way I could protect Denyse.

"It wasn't your fault."

I looked at Jamar, looking at me. "What?" I'd heard the words but didn't understand what he meant.

"I said, it's not your fault. You're thinking that all of this happened because of you, aren't you?"

"But if I hadn't been there, if we hadn't kissed, then none of this would have happened."

"That doesn't mean it was your fault," Jamar said.

I wanted to believe him, but I figured he was only saying that to make me feel better ... but why would he care how I felt?

"Jamar, did you ever have anything like this happen to you?" Denyse asked.

He scowled. "All the time."

"All the time?" I asked. That couldn't be possible. There couldn't be people like that everywhere, all the time.

"There hasn't been one time when I was dating a white girl that somebody didn't say something. Not every time we were together, but there was always at least one comment sometime."

"What sort of things?" Denyse asked.

"The usual. You've heard them all. And even worse than the things you hear them say are the things you think they're saying but you just don't hear. You see people laughing or talking and you start to think it's about you. And you feel bad for the girl you're with." He stopped and looked directly at me. "The way you feel bad for my sister and feel like it's all your fault, right?"

I nodded.

"Sooner or later you're going to hear every word under the sun, aimed at my sister, at you, at your parents. It's a matter of time. And don't think that it's only going to be out on the basketball court where somebody's going to get rough

with you," he said. "It'll be two or three guys—
maybe black or maybe white—older and bigger
than you. They'll start a fight, start pushing you
around or daring you. And the strangest thing is
that sometimes it won't even be them that starts
the fight, sometimes it'll be you."

"Me?"

"They'll say something and you'll snap and
turn around and punch somebody in the face,
even though you'll end up getting beaten up ...
you won't be able to stop yourself. Do you think
I'm wrong?"

I shook my head. I knew he was right because
I knew how mad I'd been at O'Ryan.

"It'll happen. Sooner or later," Jamar said.

We lapsed into silence. I wanted to say something but didn't know if I should. I worked up
the nerve.

"Is that why you've been giving me such a hard
time about seeing your sister?"

"That's got something to do with it."

"I thought maybe it was just because you didn't
like me."

"Who says I *do* like you?" he asked.

"No, I didn't ... sorry, I just thought that—"

"Relax," he said, and he began to laugh. "You ain't a bad guy, and you can play a little ball. She could have done worse."

"Thanks ... I guess."

"You remember Ashley, Denyse?" he asked.

"Of course I do. She was really nice and really pretty."

"And really white," Jamar added. "Do you know why we stopped seeing each other?"

"Because she was really nice and really pretty and she figured she could do better than you," Denyse said, with a small smile.

"Girl, it isn't possible to do *better* than me."

"Yeah, right, keep dreaming," Denyse said.

"I *was* dreaming," Jamar said, "and that dream turned into a nightmare." He paused. "She was the first white girl I dated, and I was the first black guy she went out with. We didn't know what to expect, like you two didn't know what to expect."

"You could have told us," Denyse said.

"And if I had, would you have believed me?"

Denyse shrugged. "I guess not. Is that why you two broke up, because of all the black and white stuff?"

"I think that was a big part of it. It sort of wore us down. It got too hard. She was my girlfriend but I couldn't hold her hand without being worried about what somebody would say or do."

"So the racists won," Denyse said.

"Maybe."

"Maybe nothing, they did win. You two broke up."

"But we probably would have broken up anyway, even if she'd been black. How many people do you know who marry the person they went out with when they were twelve or thirteen? I've gone out with other white girls since then, and other black girls, and a couple of Asian girls. None of those relationships lasted, either."

"I guess that has more to do with all of those girls discovering the real you and then finding somebody better to date," Denyse said.

"No, I think it has more to do with me realizing how many incredibly beautiful girls there are in the world, and only one of me to go around."

Denyse laughed, and that made everything suddenly seem so much better.

"And speaking of girls, I owe a couple of lucky young ladies a phone call." He started to walk away, and then stopped and turned around. "You two have to figure this out for yourselves, but I'm going to tell you what I think. You shouldn't stop seeing each other because of what some people think, or say, or do."

"We're not going to," Denyse said, and I nodded in agreement.

"Good," Jamar said. "Because you know that most of the people, almost all of the people, are really okay with you two being together. Don't forget that."

"We'll try not to," I said.

"The jerks, the racists, aren't most people, they're only some people," Jamar said. "But think about this, too. You shouldn't stay together because of those people either. Don't stay together just to prove them wrong, or because you're so pigheaded that you refuse to give in."

That made sense, especially knowing how pigheaded the two of us could be.

"Okay, Jamar," Denyse said. "I hear you."

"Good, I'm glad you can acknowledge that I am, in fact, both older *and* wiser," Jamar said.

"Well, I won't argue with the older part," Denyse said.

"If you want to remember one thing, remember this," Jamar said. "This may be about black and white, but there isn't anything black and white about it. It's all grey, shades of grey." He turned back around and left us to think about what he'd said.

"He really is a good guy … most of the time," Denyse said. "And I think he might actually like you, you know."

"I know he really does love you," I said.

"He's my brother. He's supposed to love me."

Mrs. Smith came back into the room carrying a tray with glasses and a pitcher of what looked like lemonade. She hesitated for a moment, as though not sure whether she should come in.

"Is everything okay?"

"It's okay, Mom," Denyse said, smiling. "I'm feeling better. Jamar has shared some of his *worldly wisdom* with us, and I think things are getting a bit clearer."

"Well, I am glad to hear that. It's nice to know that your brother has wisdom to spare for others. Now, where did he go?"

"He said something about having to make some phone calls to some girls."

Mrs. Smith shook her head as she sat down beside us. "I wish that boy would spend as much time on his schoolwork as he does on that phone. If he's not calling some girl, it's some girl calling him! In my time, the girls didn't do the calling or the chasing." She stopped and smiled. "Let me guess," she said, pointing a finger at Denyse, "you were the one that went chasing after Thomas?"

"Mother!"

Mrs. Smith laughed, and I heard Denyse's laugh in her voice, and when she smiled I saw Denyse's smile. She poured the lemonade into glasses.

"Thomas, my husband was wondering if you'd be joining us in church this Sunday."

"Um ... I guess I could," I stammered.

She laughed again. "I didn't mean to put you on the spot. You know you're welcome to come any time, but you never *have* to come."

"I'd like to come again sometime, but I was going to go with my parents up to the ski lodge and hit the slopes this Sunday."

"That might be better anyway," Mrs. Smith said.

Why? Because she didn't want anybody to hassle Denyse?

"I've been listening to him practising this week's sermon, and it isn't, shall we say, one of his best. Hey, maybe *I* could go skiing with you this Sunday," Mrs. Smith suggested.

"I could ask if you ... wait, you're joking, right?"

She smiled and got to her feet. "Now I should bring one of these glasses of lemonade up to Jamar. I just *love* standing there beside him when he's trying so hard to be cool on the phone."

"So you have plans for Sunday," Denyse said when her mother was gone.

"Do you want to come? You know you're always welcome!"

"I'd like to come but I can't. Church."

"That's right."

"But I don't have church on Friday night," she said, and smiled.

"What a coincidence, neither do I! Do you want to go to a movie or something?"

"That would be nice."

"I'll talk to my mom and see if she can drive us," I said.

"If she can drive us one way I'll see if my mother can drive the other way."

"Good. I'll see if Steve wants to come ... unless you want to invite Bridget."

"Let's invite them both and not tell either that the other is coming," Denyse suggested playfully.

"That works for me," I agreed.

Denyse stood up. "I should go and wash up. I must look a mess."

I reached over and grabbed her hand. "You look fine."

She tried to walk away but I held onto her hand. I wanted to say something else, but I didn't know how to put it into words.

"Denyse, when we go to the movies ... when we walk in ..."

"Yeah?"

"Well, you're my girlfriend."

"I know that."

"And I want to walk in there holding your hand ... if that's okay with you."

"Of course it's okay."

"And I know that maybe some people aren't going to be happy about that," I continued.

"You're probably right," she agreed.

"But two people will be *very* happy, and that's the only part that really matters."

Denyse gave me a smile—that same beautiful, wonderful, incredible smile that I first saw from across the gym floor. She bent down and kissed me and I kissed her back. That *was* the only part that mattered.